Joe Parente

The Timing

AF205004

Joe Parente

The Timing

Time becomes the trigger that allows the fight with manipulating mad men that show no end of greed

JustFiction Edition

Impressum/Imprint (nur für Deutschland/only for Germany)
Bibliografische Information der Deutschen Nationalbibliothek: Die Deutsche Nationalbibliothek verzeichnet diese Publikation in der Deutschen Nationalbibliografie; detaillierte bibliografische Daten sind im Internet über http://dnb.d-nb.de abrufbar.
Alle in diesem Buch genannten Marken und Produktnamen unterliegen warenzeichen-, marken- oder patentrechtlichem Schutz bzw. sind Warenzeichen oder eingetragene Warenzeichen der jeweiligen Inhaber. Die Wiedergabe von Marken, Produktnamen, Gebrauchsnamen, Handelsnamen, Warenbezeichnungen u.s.w. in diesem Werk berechtigt auch ohne besondere Kennzeichnung nicht zu der Annahme, dass solche Namen im Sinne der Warenzeichen- und Markenschutzgesetzgebung als frei zu betrachten wären und daher von jedermann benutzt werden dürften.

Coverbild: www.ingimage.com

Verlag: JustFiction! Edition ist ein Imprint der
LAP LAMBERT Academic Publishing GmbH & Co. KG
Heinrich-Böcking-Str. 6-8, 66121 Saarbrücken, Deutschland
Telefon +49 681 37 20 310, Telefax +49 681 37 20 310-9
Email: info@justfiction-edition.com

Herstellung in Deutschland:
Schaltungsdienst Lange o.H.G., Berlin
Books on Demand GmbH, Norderstedt
Reha GmbH, Saarbrücken
Amazon Distribution GmbH, Leipzig
ISBN: 978-3-8454-4506-9

Imprint (only for USA, GB)
Bibliographic information published by the Deutsche Nationalbibliothek: The Deutsche Nationalbibliothek lists this publication in the Deutsche Nationalbibliografie; detailed bibliographic data are available in the Internet at http://dnb.d-nb.de.
Any brand names and product names mentioned in this book are subject to trademark, brand or patent protection and are trademarks or registered trademarks of their respective holders. The use of brand names, product names, common names, trade names, product descriptions etc. even without a particular marking in this works is in no way to be construed to mean that such names may be regarded as unrestricted in respect of trademark and brand protection legislation and could thus be used by anyone.

Cover image: www.ingimage.com

Publisher: JustFiction! Edition
is an imprint of the publishing house
LAP LAMBERT Academic Publishing GmbH & Co. KG
Heinrich-Böcking-Str. 6-8, 66121 Saarbrücken, Germany
Phone +49 681 37 20 310, Fax +49 681 37 20 310-9
Email: info@justfiction-edition.com

Printed in the U.S.A.
Printed in the U.K. by (see last page)
ISBN: 978-3-8454-4506-9

Copyright © 2011 by the author and LAP LAMBERT Academic Publishing GmbH & Co. KG and licensors
All rights reserved. Saarbrücken 2011

THE TIMING   Joe Parente

Time becomes the trigger that allows the Rhortec Company to activate the takeover of newly contracted businesses.

Brad Warner is in the middle of experiencing mind bending horror when lives are destroyed by any means possible. Twists and turns including MURDER unfold as the battle to save his future love ignites the fight with manipulating mad men that show no end of greed.

The Timing   Chapter 1   Joe Parente

I'm half-asleep; the alarm goes off. Did I just eat a ball of cotton? I reach over with the worst headache and shut the buzzer. There is nothing worse than waking up in a hotel without a female bed warmer. With this bad taste in my mouth, who would want to?

That last double Chivas must have done it. I guess my luck has been running a little low. In fact, I can't remember how unlucky I have been lately.

I think I remember being an undesirable jerk to a woman I sat next to last night. It may have been the ice… Yeah, bad ice in that final drink; that's it. Shit.

When I asked for the position I thought my travels would lead me to the "Promised Land of Bachelorhood". Boy was I mistaken; it took as much labor to get one in the sack as it did to get a client for Rhortec.

And so, here I am alone, trying to be excited about my new client. Though, I'll tell you, this life beats the grueling 'day to day time clock' of an office. I spent three years at headquarters going out of my mind. It was a grueling experience and I hated it. I'm not the in your face, every day sort a guy.

When the available opening came up to be on the road as a salesman, it didn't take long to beg for this job. Unfortunately, the mysterious disappearance of my predecessor has kept me wondering about his reclaiming his position.

Frank was a good man. He had no family, no sisters or brothers, not even an ex-wife. I have had more ex-wives than I am proud of. That's something to not be happy about; I think.

I suppose work 'burn out' got to him and he went to the Bahamas, Mexico or somewhere. I've toasted him every night since I took over his spot. Although we were friends, Frank was a strange sort of guy. I couldn't put my finger on it. He was a little off. I could never get too close to his psyche.

The company waited thirty-five days until the word got around that they were ready to fill the position.

Rhortec is an unusual company. They are a time management firm that improves the bottom line of any client that signs the contract. This is where I come in. The office sends the leads and then using my Rhortec training, I dangle the bait in front of the buyer. Once the hook is set, Rhortec takes over and becomes the efficiency expert. With the better use of time, they can eliminate some labor and make the prospect's business much more profitable.

The fine-tuning of this process is on a need to know basis. I don't know what happens after I sign up a business. After I'm done with one, the company wants me to go on to get the next contract

My job is to present the program and get them started on the new method of management.

The tough part is to get the final approval for the contract.

Just before Frank left, I heard he had stumbled onto the secret that makes things work. All I know is that it DOES work and so far we have never lost a client. I hope Frank doesn't show up and try to re-claim his job.

I am not a magical salesman but I know how to manipulate people. They seem to like me. As a lone child, I was always able to get my way. My folks spoiled me rotten because they must have felt bad about not being able to have other siblings.

The only thing I was lousy at was putting the final on women. Before the 'end moves', they discover that I am a brat. Things always go sour from there. This mating ritual not always eluded me but there was always the lucky break. It just didn't happen often enough.

This experience taught me to be humble, but only at times. It was the last drink that usually gets the trouble started. This is why I'm alone this fine morning. At least I have the start of a grand day, with a horrible hangover and all the trimmings.

I haven't looked outside yet. Why rush it?... By the time I glanced at the clock, I realized I had better get rolling. It was 9:00am.

Feeling fortunate that I didn't cut something off after shaving, I toweled off and slid on my shorts. This hangover was worse than I thought but with a little Visine I could look into my steaming mirror and recognize myself once more.

Deciding to finally open the blinds, the bright daylight hit me like a thunder bolt. It slapped me across the forehead giving me an instant headache. This hangover was indeed, a lot worse than I had thought.

Bravely, I dialed room service; my order of tomato juice and bagel arrived in the nick of time. I had already downed a shot of my required vodka from the room bar. The second shot went into the tomato juice and I instantly felt I could possibly take on the world and possibly the opening of the dreaded drapes again.

Yes sir, it was a bright day and the smashing of bright didn't hurt so badly now.

7

Up on the tenth floor and feeling better, I braved my view of straight down. I was a little dizzy and had to step back from the precipice. Finally I got the nerve to look over the edge again.

What I saw was the hustle and bustle of life, complete with horns blasting with busier than usual traffic and the odor of the day wafting up. It filled my nostrils with grayish brown smog. Gosh, it was great to be alive!

I dressed, with the finishing touches of my favorite power tie and felt confident after checking it for the absence of food stains.

Bending down to don my shoes and socks the sudden straightening instantly told me to rise gently. Blood pressure rising to my head must have been close to the feeling that Mt. Saint Helen must have felt during the last eruption. "Oh well," I said to myself, "I'll get over it".

Recovery was quickly absorbed. Grabbing my briefcase, I hit the elevator for my appointment.

Remembering an old movie about a happy on top of the world salesman, I attempted to whistle a happy tune. Discovering for the thousandth time that I couldn't whistle, I aborted my attempt.

Thank God, I did it in time because the elevator door opened at the sixth floor and a beautiful red head entered the lift. I tried to look into her eyes but soon discovered that she was followed by a big brute of a boyfriend. He was very successful in looking directly into my eyes. Not wanting to thrash him into a pulp I quickly looked down and again tried to whistle. They got off at the next floor as I sighed with out-going breath.

The door opened at the bustling lobby as I walked sideways through the people that were lined up at the registration desk; I was glad I wouldn't have to check out for a couple of days so I headed toward the bell man.

"Good morning sir, may I assist you?" He asked.

"Yes, you can call for a cab," I said.

"Certainly sir," He replied with an English accent. "It will take a few moments sir."

"That's fine. I'm early anyway." I looked at my watch. "I'm quite early."

Deciding what to do next, I took in the expanse of the lobby. It was a very large open room with beautiful decor. The walls were painted in an exciting business mural of a busy downtown city with the vanishing point of Times Square as a focal point. Around the mural, were men with top hats reminding me of the early 1900's complete with trolley cars and horse drawn carriages. It had the look of commerce in a much kinder way than what takes place in today's world.

I have often wished I could have lived during those times. If I had lived then knowing what I know now about business, I am sure that in no time, wealth would shine my way.

I walked over to the coffee bar and ordered a large cup, but then decided to help myself to three spoons of sugar to add to the black liquid. I knew that this was going to make me feel a lot better than I did a half hour ago. The sweet cup did exactly that and I was grateful.

As I looked through the windows at the downtown area, things outside were really starting to pop. Hustle and bustle, cabs, luggage and town cars were everywhere. People were clamoring to go somewhere. You could tell that the patience of some was running thin each time the crowd or heavy traffic blocked someone's way.

I hated it but I still loved it. There is nothing like the anticipated high of getting and closing my first sale for the company.

Just as I had finished with my coffee, the bell man motioned that my cab had arrived. It was exactly like all the others, as I peered through the glass doors of the hotel, a bright yellowish-orange Checker Cab was impatiently ready to take me away. I handed a couple of bucks to the bell man as I walked out of the automatic opening of heavy glass doors.

As soon as I had stepped off of the last entry step something happened!
The surrounding sky that filtered through the buildings was black, and as I looked around everything was now at night! What the hell! I was only a few steps from the cab and the only light that I could see was the dim light bulbs of the closed business up and down the street.

What was a very busy metro New York was now a row of closed store fronts and not a sole around? "What the hell!" I muttered quietly to myself in disbelief.

9

I couldn't have had this bad of a hang-over for this to happen. "Could I?" I said to myself. I felt my arms as a little nervous sweat started on my forehead" What the hell?"

Twisting back to take a look, the darkness enveloped me. It looked as though the hotel was out of business. No light penetrated the glass. I could not see anyone or anything inside the pitch-black hotel opening. Totally confused, I pushed at the doors. The doors opened! I stepped inside the threshold.

As soon as my whole body passed the double, heavy glass door, it was as if someone had turned on all the lights. "What is going on with me?" I thought to myself. It was as if, well, as if things were as I had left them. That peaceful mural was there, the crowded lobby was a buzz and the bell man was at his corner.

"I have never experienced anything like that before," I said, under my breath.

The bell man walked over "Did you not get your taxi sir?"

"Uh, no, I forgot something in my room," I said, feeling embarrassed about what had happened.

I spun around and looked out at the bright new day.

"Are you alright sir?" asked the bell man.

Red faced, I said "Sure I'm fine, just getting my bearings." I moved off to the elevator as I noticed from the corner of my eye the bell man following me with his eyes.

Not knowing what just happened, not sure I wanted to know, I made the only decision that was possible, a quick detour to the bar and a straight shot to calm my nerves. It was still close to nine. The appointment was not for a couple of hours, so I had just enough time to get my head straight…

The quick fix seemed to help as I walked through the crowd again.

"There you are sir may I call you another cab?" asked the bell man.

"Yes, please, and thank you for being so patient," I answered nervously.

"Glad to be of assistance sir," he said, as I handed him a buck.

A short time later, I got the high sign that my transportation had arrived. Making my way to the doors, I looked outside, this time with a little buzz from the booze, I walked onto the street.

Dark! Everything was dark! Up and down the street was night filled darkness! I was frightened! "What the hell is going on?" I said loudly "This is silly, this must be a trick. Am I asleep? Is this a nightmare?"

The outline of the cab could barely be seen from the reflection from a closed cigar shop's neon sign. There the taxi stood, in the middle of its lane…waiting.

Starting to become accustomed to the night, my sight began to improve. Just moments ago, I was exposed to a very bright day. As I approached the vehicle I looked into its side window but could not see a thing. All was black. I stepped back, wanting to run, but to where? Feeling my knees weaken, I turned to look at the dimness of the hotel entrance. I felt the blood drain from my face, as I tried to make some sense of it all. Reaching for the door handle on the taxi to steady myself, I pulled on its lever trying to gain some footing, the door opened. I fell inside, as scorching pain hit my brain with an instant sun drenched bright beacon of daylight.

I heard a voice "Where to sir?" The driver said as he looked straight ahead "Where to?" He repeated

I couldn't answer. He turned to me, "sir?" He looked at me. "Sir, are you okay?"

I couldn't answer. "Sir, you don't look so good… You okay?"

All I could do was to stare at the busy, brightly lit street with people rushing here and there.

He continued. "Hey you, you okay? Where do you want to go?"

"Better let me out, I don't feel well," I muttered

"Well get the hell out! Jesus, you fuckers think I got all day to waste my time!" He cussed. "Hey buddy, what the hell is wrong with you anyway?"

I couldn't answer but managed to open the taxi door to a black night sky. Stumbling out, I was able to make my way back to the closed looking hotel. The doors opened and I was again exposed to its daylight.

Unable to make it all the way into the lobby, the bell man rushed over to help. "Are you alright sir? You look pale sir. Please sit here." He indicated a chair close to the entry. "May I get you some water?"

"I'm, a, a, sure." I said.

"Yes sir I will right back. Is there someone I can call for you?" He snapped his fingers to a subordinate and made the appropriate gestures.

"Thank you, I think I'll need to get to my room" Rising from the chair.

He laid his hand on my shoulder, "one moment sir, here is that water."

I took in a sip. "Thanks that helped, I need to get to my room now. I must have had a heck of a time last evening, or maybe some bad ice in my drink. That's it some bad ice."

My knuckles were white as I relinquished my grip on the briefcase I had forgotten about. "I'm fine, thanks," I said. As I got up, I made my way to the elevators and managed to press the button for the tenth floor.

......

"I don't know what I ate last night but I'm not well. I feel like hell," I explained to the Rhortec operator.

"Well Brad, I mean Mr. Warner, I think you need to talk to the boss. I'll get you to Mr. Rhoram. Are you sure that you didn't party all night, Brad?"

"No, really Becky," I struggled to explain, "It was something I had eaten I'm pretty sure of it." She knew me like a book. I've tried to get in her pants while I worked the 'time clock' at the office but so far—

"I'm connecting you now Mr. Warner," she transferred the call.

"Problem Mr. Warner?" asked Willhelm Rhoram.

"Hi Will, sorry to bother you with this but I am sick," I tried to speak honestly.

"What is the problem Brad? You know this is your first call on the road." I could tell he was agitated.

"I know sir." I quickly dropped the informal, 'Will,' greeting. "I was just about on my way when it hit me. I was in the cab when I became, well, unable to continue, so I had to come back to the room. I have to sit today out sir."

"What time was your appointment Brad?" He was not softening.

12

"Just before noon sir," I stated.

"Did you call to cancel?" He snorted.

I answered apologetically. "Not yet sir, I wanted to call you first."

"Well hop to it man, we sell time programs here and I expect all my people to be on the second. I went through the importance of time management with you at your training. We, as a company cannot expect our clients to believe our program if our employees do not adhere to the basic principles. Be efficient; make that call to your potential as soon as we hang up. Understood?"

"Yes sir, I will." I felt as though I had been put through the ringer.

"Good, and get better." He hung up.

He was a tough old bird, but I had to give him credit. He started this company about ten years ago and it has been very successful. The company is now trading big on the stock market and its value has grown considerably. Although Rhorem's bedside manner was always a bit rough, he was able to bring in some talented people. I haven't met all of the talent, especially the latest CTA (computer time analysis) that seemed to control the main lab in the company.

In my three years prior to going on the road, things have been tight-mouthed. Any questions about details were directed to the old man. He brushed off most queries as 'a need to know' situation. It was best not to ask. They paid very well; why should I rock the boat?

Looking up the telephone number of the missed appointment, Baetacom Incorporated, I was able to re-set for tomorrow at 11:00 in the morning.

Swearing off booze, I hit the sack.

Awakened for the second time today by a shrill ringing of the telephone, I grabbed the alarm to check out the time of 1:00 PM. "Hello, this is Brad." I was half awake.

"Hey buddy, get out of bed."

"Who is this?" I asked, with a rusty voice.

"It's me, Brad, get up I need to meet with you."

"Frank, Jesus man I thought you were dead!" I was thinking I was dreaming.

"It's me, and I'm not dead." He was speaking urgently. "I have to meet you; I'll see you in the bar in ten minutes." He hung up.

Jumping up from bed, I started to mentally examine this day. What else could happen, First, I couldn't score, second, I hallucinate with the worst hangover I have ever had and third after almost getting fired over the telephone, my job will be replaced by Frank, the missing pal. Shit!

Wearing jeans and a T-shirt, I took the elevator to the lobby bar. Just as I expected, Frank was sitting at the back booth, I noticed him instantly as I approached. "I can't believe this Frank, is it you?"

"Hello Brad, we've got to talk!" speaking more urgent than ever.

"Ok, what is going on?" My eyes were twice as big as they should be.

"What happened to your appointment this morning?" he asked.

"How do you know about that?" I rubbed an eye. "We thought you were dead."

"Brad, I don't have much time but I will answer your questions soon. Now what happened to your appointment this morning?"

Bewildered, I answered with the first thing that came into my head. "I got sick and missed it, why?"

He continued. "You cannot miss these appointments."

"You are sounding like the old man. I just got reamed by him this morning." I remembered the conversation, I had with the boss. "Why would you care about my appointments?"

"I can't explain that now but I assure you that it is all tied together. If you miss the appointments the company makes for you, shit will hit the fan!" He was serious.

"Do you still work for this company? Or did you come back to take my job?" I awaited the answer.

"No," he said, "On both questions. What is most important, are the appointments. I missed one once without calling to change it. Did you call to change yours?"

14

"Yeah he insisted on it," I said quickly. "Please tell me what is going on. I've had a terrible day," I said, pleading.

"I can't tell you any more now. The time is not right. In a way, we are being watched," he said as he looked around. "At least I know you are."

"What? -Why. What the hell are you talking about?"

"Look, all I can tell you now, is that there is more to this job than signing up a client. You have to keep your appointments and you have to be on time. Most important, be on time. When were you supposed to meet the client this morning?"

"Before noon," I said.

He wrinkled his forehead "You have to be more specific than that. Rhortec Inc. is always specific about exact appointment times. Look at your itinerary. I am sure that there is a written, to the second, time. What time did you expect to be there? For your own sake, be accurate now."

I looked at the ceiling trying to remember specifics. "I was going to get there a little early, so I could, you know, research them first."

"For Christ sakes, don't you remember your training about being on time and never late or early? You have to be exact or you will screw things up real bad you idiot!"

I stood up "What gives you the gall to talk to me that way, If you knew what I have gone through today you"—

He broke in. "Did you leave the building before your planned timing?"

"Yeah?" quizzically, I answered.

"Were things a little off?" He asked.

"Were they ever?" I was still enraged. "And things were all closed outside, I mean, it looked like nighttime!"

"Keep your voice down." He gestured with his palms. "I have got to get out of here; you might have been over heard."

"Hey wait I can't believe this is happening. You mean I wasn't hallucinating about the night and closed stores and the"-

"No, you weren't". He looked around. "I gotta' go I don't want to be discovered. I'll be in touch soon. Meanwhile just do your damn job."

"But you need to answer some questions."

"Later." He held a hand up like a traffic cop, and was gone.

I stood there with my mouth open. I needed a drink and fast. I have never felt so totally in the dark as I have at this minute. Something was definitely wrong.

At least one thing was good to me last night: me. Not over doing it, I didn't hunt the elusive two-legged dear. Keeping me out of trouble had some rewards. The most important one, I didn't have a headache. It was 7: AM, and plenty of rest was absorbed. For once, this coming of a brand new day was welcomed. I was in a good mood despite the turmoil that I had been through the previous morning. I still had many questions that were still unanswered, I had decided to do my job as Frank had suggested. It was kind of a survival thing I guess. I did have to keep the paychecks coming in.

I had plenty of time to go over my plan to nail the next customer, so I started to study them. Reading up on the portfolio that Rhortec had supplied went well with the large breakfast that room service had delivered and I only spilled about a pint of coffee on my work.

With my eye on the clock, my sober brain had arranged the perfect framework of time to walk into the client's office. I am sure that this was going to be a perfect day.

The company I had to visit at eleven was a small one with a large potential. The CEO and founder was William Foster with about ninety employees.

The company, Baetacom, was a very friendly family owned business. It seemed that William's wife, son and daughter were the headliners. They specialized in cell messaging, an up and coming field. The problem was the competition, or at least too much competition. If cell messaging was orange juice, the competition was like adding too much water to the mix. No one got a good glass. I could see that they needed help in improving profits from the Rhortec program. I looked forward to our meeting.

It was getting to that time when the elevator ride to the lobby was due, so off I go with my Rhortec supplied briefcase. Clean tie and shiny shoes, what could be better than that. Whistling perhaps? Nah, never could whistle.

Here we are in the lobby, as I ordered the cab from the bell man. He showed his concern for which I was grateful.

As soon as the taxi showed, I was up and at it and ready to leave the building. I was right on with the schedule. I reached for the door with a little apprehension of yesterday's unusual happenings. Stepping onto the street I looked back through the hotel windows and noticed the bell man with a smile, he was looking directly at me.

It was a pure beautiful bright morning. The traffic was busy as were the pedestrians. I got into the cab and the driver asked "Where to sir."

"Do you know where Baetacom Inc. is located?" I was looking in the portfolio.

"Yes sir, about fifteen minutes from here." He looked at me in his mirror.

"Well that's fine; I have to be there right at 11:00." I checked my watch.

He assured me, "no problem sir."

The cab pulled up at the correct time and I got out and paid the fare. Two at a time, I took the steps and proceeded to present my card to the receptionist.

"Mr. Foster is expecting you, please follow me." She had the nicest ass, so following her was an exciting task.

We walked to his office and Judy, I asked her name, introduced me. "Mr. Foster, this is your 11: AM, this is Mr. Warner." We shook hands.

He read my card. "Come right in Brad, would you like coffee?"

"That would be refreshing, thank you." He gestured to a seat next to his desk.

"Coffee, please Judy." He had pressed the intercom button.

"I hope all is well with you today Brad, I got a follow up call from your boss, uh, Mr. Rhorem. He told me that you had eaten something that had made you sick. Are you okay now?"

Judy entered with a tray. "There you are dad."

I took a double take. "Thank you."

"Brad?" Mister Foster caught me with a smile as I took the cup from her.

I was surprised that the old man had called him. "Excuse me, much better today sir."

He said quickly. "Please, call me Bill." He scooted into his chair "Well please tell me more about your company."

Being poor at canned spiels, I explained the program. "Well Mr. Fos- I mean Bill, we as a company have been in existence and have been able to stay in existence because we believe in making your company more money. When you win, we win. You could almost say that we create a marriage with the sole intent for you to create more profit. The bottom line is quite an important thing for companies such as yours do you agree?" I took a sip of coffee.

"Well of course Brad, go on."

"We do this in a way that will let you control your own company and still reap the benefits through the use of our knowledge of time management. We have on our staff world-renowned experts that will put in place a comprehensive program that will enable you to reach your dream goals. By the careful study of the workings of your company, our experts will find ways to increase efficiency so that labor costs will be reduced. The qualities of your finished products or programs are not compromised in any way. Of course, all of this comprehensive study is done on a complete confidential way; we will never jeopardize your company secrets or other things that you want to keep private."

"What is required of me to get things started?" His interest peaked.

"All we ask is that you follow our direction to the letter. There can be no variation, except for changes that you can make with our approval." I was coming in for the kill.

"Wait now, it sounds as though you will be taking over my company," he said nervously.

"On the contrary, Bill, you have complete control at all times. You alone will reap the benefits; you alone will spend your new profits. We have never lost a client. Companies that sign up with us continue to grow beyond their expectations. What do you say Bill? Wouldn't you like to take your company to the next step?" I waited for an answer.

"Look Brad, I know that we have had our problems. I know that something needs to happen to keep us on the razors edge. If you don't mind, I would like to look at your contract. I would like to run this by my wife."

Attempting to use my trained closing techniques, I said, "Does your wife always make your decisions sir?"

"Of course not."

I felt the closing. "Well if she does not make the important decisions, what is to stop you from those dreams you had when you started this company?"

"Well I"-

I continued, "You know Bill, I took the liberty to fill out everything on this contract." I pulled the paper work from my briefcase. "And all you have to do is to sign right here." I pointed to the signature line.

Hesitantly, he looked as though he was being rushed. "What if I don't like the program?"

"If ever we do not do what we promise in the way of increasing your business, we will be required to correct the situation within ninety days. The ninety days starts upon your notification. If at that time business does not grow as we state in this agreement, we will relinquish the contract. The better your company does, the better we do. It is as simple as that."

"It sounds good, let me read." He gestured with an open palm.

"Here you are Bill. I handed him the documents. "Say, do you have any more of that coffee?"

Bill took the contract. "Sure Brad, if you don't mind, just see my daughter in front. That will give me some time to read this over."

Leaving him alone with the contract, I felt confident that things were going very well, in fact extremely well. I walked to the reception area. "Hello Judy, your father sent me in for more coffee."

"Certainly, Mister—"

"Please, Brad, if you don't mind," I interrupted with a smile.

"Certainly, Brad," she said, giving the most beautiful glance.
"How long have you worked for your dad?" I prodded.

"Let's see, about six years, I'd say. How long have you worked for your company, Brad?" She poured coffee.

"Over six years." I lied.

"Do you like to travel?" she asked.

"Yes it is exciting at times." Noticing her ring-less finger, "I am new in town and have a yearning to explore a little of New York. Would you be free for dinner?"

"I'm sorry, Brad. I have made it a policy not to mix personal things with business."

I felt like a turd for asking. I should have waited until she knew me better. My luck with women was in line with all the other times that I have tried. "Please don't close the door on me so fast, perhaps another time?"

She smiled. "I'll see."

Bill's voice came over the intercom. "Send Brad in please, Judy."

I overheard the page and quickly rose to leave but not before thanking Judy for the coffee.

I entered the office. "Yes sir?"

"I have been looking this over and have a few questions. You're asking us to give you complete dossiers on all employees, and especially family members. May I ask why?"

"Yes Bill, as you know, the fastest way to cut costs is to make sure that you are paying for what you get for your labor force. Now I'm not saying that we plan to cut anyone, but there may be some re-assignments. This would enable us to take a very close look at time management. Using your labor force properly will definitely add to the bottom line. In order to make some of these decisions palatable to your employees; you may switch that burden to this new management program. I will assure you Bill, any decisions that are made will be very humane and with your company's feelings in mind." I spouted all this from the purest section of the Rhorem training manual. I impressed myself!

"How about my son, he has a hefty position here. He may not be too happy about me sharing personal information."

Assuring him, I continued, "Bill, please let me make our intentions clear. Anything we do is to better your firm. We are here to make your company shine. All of this information is necessary to get a true picture of Baetacom so you can buy your new yacht." I said this as we both smiled.

"Brad, I usually like to run this by my wife and family but a re-vamping is needed. The best way to accomplish this is to do it now. Your program sounds good and too many different decisions will spoil the broth. Here are your signed documents. Let's get the ball rolling. I will have all the information ready for you in two days. Why don't you come back on Monday? I'll work on it this weekend."

What a rush! "Fine sir, I'll be here at the same time Monday to pick up the batch of paperwork, Thank you Bill!" Standing, I took his hand with an enthusiastic grip.

On the way out I gave Judy an exaggerated wink and promised to see her Monday. I started to ask her out again but felt that I should wait until next week. Why should I break the lucky streak? Leaving the office I felt like doing a double heel kick, I was stoked! Oh, the hell with protocol, I went back in and told Judy that I was staying at the Walton if she decided to change her mind.

Making my way to the street, I flagged down a cab and told the cabby that I needed to make two stops. The first one was to overnight the contract to the main office and the second one was to go to the hotel to celebrate in the bar.

Doors opened on the lobby floor as the melee' of noise hit me. There was the piano bar, the clinking of glassware and the buzz of over a hundred people talking at the same time. This is where the action is and I'm geared up. Walking into the bar, I noticed my favorite bell man looking my way with that helpful smile. Walking over to him I realized that I did not know his name.

"Hello Mister Warner, how are you doing today? You look very nice this evening sir."

"Well thank you I had a tough beginning, say, what is your name? After all of your help I realized that I didn't know your name."

"It is Jules sir, may I be of assistance this evening?"

I thought to myself, what a perfect name for this guy. "No Jules, I thought I would enjoy the scenery here tonight."

"Very good sir, please be careful of the bad ice." He walked away.

Now how the hell-- was that a co-incidence, how did he know about my alleged affair with bad ice? I don't think I told him anything about ice, did I? I shuffled off to the bar.

"What will you have sir?" asked the bartender.

"Hi, I'll have a scotch and soda please." I laid a twenty on the bar.

"Sure."
"Any particular brand sir?"
"Sure, make it Chivas."

23

Sipping on my first one I surveyed the surroundings and noticed a red head in the corner. It looked like she was by herself so I sent over whatever she was drinking. I wanted to make sure that she knew where the drink came from. She looked up and acknowledged me by tipping her glass just as a big brute sat in next to her.

"Shit." I said under my breath.

"Another sir?" The bartender asked.

"You bet and make it a double." I thought to myself. *Boy, can I pick 'em.*

Drink after drink and trying to drum up a conversation with someone, I started to get a little hungry, so I asked for a menu.

"Would you like to dine in the restaurant sir?" the bartender asked.

"Yeah I think I better, there is no action for me in here." Standing up, I was led to the dining room. Getting all my meals through room service, this was a new room to me.

As I began to check out the menu that the dining waiter handed me, I could see that eating in the room had caused me to miss some wonderful entrées. Everything sounded great. I guess that my hunger was beginning to show. I looked out at the doorway to catch my waiter's eye when I had noticed that Jules was smiling my way. What kind of hours was he working? It seems as though he had been here every minute... Strange.

The waiter appeared out of nowhere and startled me. "Have you decided yet sir?"

I jumped, "Yea, let me try the rib eye. Medium rare. I'll have that with baked potato and a large dinner salad with blue cheese dressing." I knew I couldn't go wrong with that.

"A terrific choice sir, you will enjoy that." He attempted to take the menu; I noticed the printing on the back and I held it back. "Would there be anything else sir?"

"Not at this time, but if you don't mind, may I read the menu a little longer?"

"Certainly sir." He departed.

I did not believe what I was reading because on the back of the menu in small print was 'A Rhortec company'. Now that was one for the books! Rhortec owned this place! No wonder the company was so adamant about my staying here. No wonder there were no limits to the expenses, this was already paid for by them. I was un-aware that the Old Man was in the restaurant business.

The waiter brought the salad and I ordered a single to go along with dinner. As he was setting the plate, I asked, "do you know who owns this place?"

"No sir, about two years ago a large company from California took us over. Before that, this place had almost gone out of business, but since the new company"—he paused, "well look at it sir, we have been busy all the time."

I enjoyed my meal, had a couple more drinks, wobbled up to my room and crashed.

The telephone rang very loud at 8: AM. My head was about to explode, all I wanted to do was sleep. Why me, "Yeah, who is it?"

"Hi bud, this is Frank. It's time to talk again."

"For Christ's sake Frank, this is Saturday morning. You keep waking me up. Have you ever thought of calling at a decent hour?" I was pissed.

"Brad, it's 8: AM, that's not too early. Can we meet at the bar? It's for your own good. I have something that has come up."

Mellowing, "Oh, alright, about ten minutes?"

"You got it, don't be late."

I met him at the same seat as last time. On the way in, I ran into Jules with that same helpful smile. I brushed by him, but I could feel his eyes on my back. "What's up, Frank?"

"You look like crap this morning," he said. He gave me the once over.

"Thanks Frank, that helps my mood." I sat opposite of him at the table.

"That booze is gonna kill you."

"Ok Dad, what's up?"

He leaned closer to me. "I just got word that Rhortec swallowed up a company that I had sold for them. It seems that the company eliminated some essential people and replaced them with their own. Something had happened to the CEO and according to the contract they signed, Rhortec made some decisions that caused a 'take over'."

"What happened to the CEO, Frank?" I was awake now.

"I'm not sure; we are looking into it now."

25

I was fully awake now. "We, Frank, Who the hell are we?"

"I can only tell you this so far, I am an investigator for the trade commission and some things don't add up with Rhortec. I was recruited by the Feds shortly before I left my position with Willhelm Rhorem. I had to leave him and make it seem like a disappearing act in order to get the ball rolling. I can't tell you anything else right now but I will be in contact. We don't have anything on them now but something is fishy."

"Wow you said a mouthful. I found out last night that Rhortec also owns this hotel."

"Yeah, I know." He started to rise.

"Wait, I have many questions."

"I know you do but I have got to go. When is your next meeting?"

"At eleven on Monday. It's at Baetacom. I have to pick up papers to follow through with my sale."

"Congratulations on that. I'll tell you what, I'll pick you up at 11:45 outside the office. That should give you enough time to complete your task."

"Ok, but"- He started to walk away.

"That's all for now." He said. "I'll see you then."

All I could see was his back and a glimpse of Jules, staring at me with that sickening smile. He looked away quickly upon my discovery. Was it my imagination that I felt that Jules was watching something, or he was watching me.

This was enough for right now, the headache was back and I was confused. I knew I had to do something about it so I headed for the bar for an ice cold beer.

26

The remainder of the day was a blur. After a few toddies, I managed to have lunch. It was becoming a little disconcerting to try to understand all the information that Frank was giving me. Trying to weigh my options, I realized that I still had a job to do, so I went back to work. It was about 4:o'clock when I went back to my room. When I got there, the light was blinking on the message center. Curious, I retrieved a recording through the operator. Not surprised, it was from the office, but it was urgent. The secretary had left Will's cell number so that I could call as soon as possible. The call had come in at 3:00PM. I dialed.

"Rhorem, here." The Old Man sounded like he was in his usual form.

"Hi Will, this is Brad." I was trying to be jovial.

"Brad, that contract you sent is not complete. Now I know you are new at this but I must have all the 'I's dotted and the 'T's crossed on these." He sounded a little put out.

"I'm sorry boss. What did I forget?"

"It's an initial. You forgot to get him to initial the paragraph about the ninety-day notice in case we need to give his account a little more attention. You may think that this is not something to worry about but if things get nasty, we would need that initial for back-up." He sounded like my father.

"I can get that done at 11:o'clock on Monday. You could send that contract back and I'll get it done, sorry for the screw-up."

"Let's concentrate on the P&Ls you have to get first. You can make another trip back in the week to get it done. I'm coming out there on Monday to take care of some business and want to meet up with you. If your appointment is at 11:00 then you should be free at 1:00 PM ok?" That made me nervous. "I can bring out the contract then so you can fix your mistake."

"Sure mister Rhorem, that will be fine." Boy, this is all I needed, more crap to worry about, "That will work out well. Do I meet you at the hotel?"

"Of course! Be there at 1:00PM on the dot. How is the study coming on that printer company?"

"Real good so far sir." I lied. "The report is very comprehensive as usual."

"Just get the deal, see you Monday." He hung up.

That guy was sure an ass. I could hardly wait to see him on Monday 'Be there at 1:00'. Nice guy!

It looks as though my Sunday will be busy studying for my next sales call. I didn't even know the name of the company. I'm lucky he didn't ask. I probably should have at least looked at it. Oh well.

Not all this good news from the boss even made me thirsty. Now that was something. I was getting tired of being crapped on so I decided to look at Quick Print's company portfolio. About five minutes of that and I fell asleep.

If I had a dream that night I didn't know it because I was awakened at 6: AM by some noise in the hallway. It was probably some guy coming in from having the best sex from some gal that I wished I had. All I could think about was Judy at Baetacom. She was a beauty and I was going to see her tomorrow. It would be nice to make some headway with her. I liked her, and she did have a great ass. I put my hands behind my head and stared at the ceiling as I said to myself: "Yes sir a great ass."

Getting out of bed, I jumped in the shower, did my duty and shaved. I wanted to get a good start for my meeting Monday. Breakfast was on my mind. I could then get down to reading the required material on the printing outfit.

The door opened at the lobby and right in front of me was Jules. I acknowledged with a nod and kept right on walking towards the breakfast bar. This guy was starting to creep me out. I ordered a Bloody Mary and a newspaper. I finished and went back to the room.

Getting into the information about 'Quick Print', I discovered that they were a company with twelve locations. The main office was located in the New York outskirts. Their business looked a little soft; in fact, it mirrored the same picture as Baetacom. The potential was there. Trimming down the labor could help with their failing profits. The troublesome thing that stuck out in my mind was that they owned most of their locations. However, not knowing the city that well, I couldn't tell how good those locations were. They were doing about five million but with their sixty-five employees, taxes, utilities and medical, I could see some room for improvement.

I kept on reading and got the true flavor of the problems that faced this company. I looked into the ownership and circumstances of the twenty-year-old firm. I also wondered how the Old Man got all this information. Someone did his or her homework! Rhortec must be dialed in somewhere. Some of this stuff looked as though it was highly confidential.

With a couple more hours of study, this one seemed like a slam-dunk, so I kept reading.

My eyeballs were getting tired. As I glanced at the clock, I saw it was 5: PM! I could not believe that I had been at this all day. It was time for a break. The hostess had re-stocked the room bar so I helped myself to a beer and ordered dinner over the telephone.

Morning came early, but that was fine. There was plenty to do today. Ordering coffee, I mentally refreshed today's schedule. One thing having to be sure of was to memorize all the data about The Quick Print Company. I was almost positive a quizzing was coming from the Old Man at 1: PM, let me rephrase that, 1:00 PM. I just had a great idea! If I could get a new contract signed with Bill initialing the proper places, the boss would probably forgive me for the past over-sight. I'm brilliant! Having some time to kill, I studied more about Quick Print.

After finishing that refresher course, I filled out a new contract to present to Bill at Baetacom. All that was needed now were the signatures. The most important thing to do today was to see Judy again. I'll try to come on a little less strong this time. Maybe I'll get to home base.

It was time to go, so I ordered a cab to meet out front in ten minutes. Everything was working without a hitch and I was on my way.

I arrived at Judy's desk right at 11: AM. She was as glad to see me as I was her. She informed me that her dad had a meeting at 11:30 so I rushed in to see him. She asked me to stop by her office on the way out; she had something to tell me. That sounded great!

"Hi Bill." I reached over as he rose to shake hands.

"How are you Brad?"

"Fine sir."

He picked up an arm full of papers and he put them into a jumbo envelope. "It took me through Saturday to get this together. "Everything should be here to get you started."

"I appreciate all your hard work Bill." I lifted the heavy package from him. "There was a mistake on my part when you signed that contract Bill. To save time, I was wondering if you could re-do this one for me. It's the same paperwork." I showed him the copy of the original. "I had forgotten to have you initial this paragraph here." I pointed to the spot. "I have written 'void' on this copy and signed it, so if you could please"--

"No problem Brad, I know how these things are, besides your boss called and made mention that you would be bringing one by sometime this week. We might as well get it done earlier." He completed the new one and handed it back. "There you are Brad. Now if you will excuse me, I have an appointment across town." We shook hands again. "Call me as soon as things get underway. Sorry that we don't have time to talk right now."

"Of course Bill." I walked out to Judy's desk.

She indicated a chair. "Thank you for stopping Brad. The reason that I wanted to talk to you was that—well it concerns my brother. He was a little put out when he learned that dad had signed a contract with your company. I just wanted to make you aware that my brother needs a little extra care. That is, he somewhat flies off the handle when he is not consulted about affairs of this company. When my Dad retires, my brother Jeff will take over the company, and he seems very protective of things." She seemed so sweet in her 'matter of fact' comments.

Speaking sincerely, I wanted to assure her. "I understand, Judy, I'll do whatever I can to let him know the honesty of Rhortec."

"Thank you Brad, this will also help you accomplish your goals." She smiled that beautiful way.

"You know Judy, when I came back, I thought that you were going to say something else."

She started to frown. "What was that Brad?"

"I thought that you were going to tell me that you would accept a dinner invitation from me." I was looking at her with 'puppy dog eyes'. "Well?"

She paused "You have a vivid imagination, don't you Brad?"

"If I was not interested in you, I wouldn't have asked you to have dinner with me." I was letting it all hang out.

Sounding a little interested in me she said: "I have been so busy with work and all that I just haven't had a lot of time to think about it. What type of food do you like?" She was getting warm. "I mean if you would like to meet after work sometime, I guess that I could."

Wow! That's the best news that has happened to me yet. Feeling over-whelmed, I suddenly did not know what to say.

"Brad?"

"Yes-yes. We could have a nice dinner out and we could get to know each other." I sounded like a school kid on his first date.

"Tell me more about yourself Brad. I have some time right now to learn a little about you." She was looking with the most wonderful eyes.

We talked and laughed together for a while. Things were going very well. My joking personality was causing her to laugh. I finally felt very comfortable with her, and I could tell that the same was happening to her.

She talked about a boyfriend she had in college. She had dated him for a full year. Things got serious and eventually they married. That is when her trust in men fell to the bottom rung. They were married for a total of a year and a half. The trust she had for him eroded severely when infidelity took hold. They ended up in a divorce in which her father bailed her out with a quick settlement. She did not expound on that and I did not ask. I felt better about the background explanation from me, since we had both gone through some tough times. This girl really interested me.

I glanced at the clock, it was almost noon and I was going to be late. "Is that the right time? If it is, I am in trouble. I would much rather talk with you but I have to go."

"Ok, call me here at the office, bye Brad."

I hated to leave, just when things were going my way. "I'm sorry I have to go, I promise to call you." I left in a run.

31

Pushing open the door of the office building, I was able to catch the cab that Frank was in. "Sorry Frank, made it as soon as I could."

Frank looked pissed. "Jesus Brad, remember me asking you not to be late?" He was pointing his finger. "Don't ever be late with anything the company has you do. You will be in trouble. You'd be playing with fire if this had been a sanctioned appointment. Let's go get a cup of coffee around the corner." He slapped me on the shoulder treating me like a teacher scolding a young schoolboy.

Apologetically, "Sorry Frank it couldn't be helped. Listen, Old Man Rhorem called and he is in town, he wants to meet at 1:o'clock today. Do I have enough time to get to the hotel?"

"I don't know Brad it's going to be tight. What the hell does he want to see you about?" Frank sounded anxious.

"It's about the contract that I had gotten from the last sale."

"You didn't screw that up did you?" His eyes opened in disbelief.

"It was a small thing Frank. It was a forgotten initial on a paragraph." I tried to make the excuse.

Frank was being very adamant. "Don't you know by now that there are no small things with this outfit? One has to be very careful to follow all the rules. We are not going to have time for that coffee, we better get back so that you don't miss him." We drove back to the hotel. "Now if we get there early you need to wait in the cab until the exact time." Frank turned to the cabby. "Let me off two blocks before we get to the Walton Hotel." Frank turned to me. "I don't want anyone to see me."

The cab arrived early. "Now remember, wait until it's time." Frank got out well ahead of our arrival.

Suddenly, realization set in, I forgot my briefcase with the paper work, contract and all information that needs to be turned in to Rhorem. Shit-Shit-Shit! I leaned over to the cabby. "Can you get me back to the place where you picked me up?" Sweat broke out on my forehead. "I forgot something at Baetacom. You will have to get me back here at 1:PM sharp. Can you do it?"

The cab driver scratched his head at the same time looked at his trip- timer clock on the dash. "Man, you aksin a lot, maybe we can, maybe we don't. Gonna' cost ya extra twenty, but I give 'er hell.

"Rush, please." The sweat was building.
The drive was hellish, but it looked like the driver made it. On the return trip, however, traffic got in our way and if I was lucky, I would only be about ten minutes late. "Thanks, I think that this will be fine." I handed him forty bucks and opened the door of the taxi.

A piano hit me. At least it felt like it. As soon as stepping out of the cab, the sky, the road, the surroundings, all black. The shock hit once more; I felt sick. "Not this again, please not this!" My hand had left the taxi door handle and when I tried to re-establish a grip, it was gone. The cab, the driver, my briefcase, all gone! When the cab driver stopped, he was right in front of the hotel. I could not see anything now. Slowly my eyes became accustomed to the dark. I could feel the irises' of my eyeballs open wide. It felt as though they were as large as manhole covers trying to gather as much light as possible. It was too much for my brain to comprehend. Stumbling on something, I must have hit my head. The sharp pain above the eyebrow brought me to my senses. I could feel warm sticky fluid dripping down my cheek. Reaching up, I touched it with my finger and I tasted blood.

Out of the corner of my eye, I noticed the word 'Cigars' spelled out in neon window sign. It gave an eerie reflection. I had seen that same sign earlier. I thought that the first time that this happened was the result of a horrible hangover. I knew that this time was different. I had not been drinking. Focusing on the sign it seemed to move away as if it were involved in a constant vanishing point getting further and further away. Since it was the only source of light, I started to walk after it. I picked up my pace and soon started into a run. Fear had me running in the dark, but I still was not able to catch up with it. The image did not completely disappear. Its radiance was bouncing a reflection off a narrow passageway.

With that minute amount of glow, I realized that the reflection was from the walls of an alley. I must have wandered into it as I was following the red neon's eerie glow. Not knowing much about New York, one thing was sure, the place not to be in this city was a dark alley.

Alphonso had been a cab driver in New York for three years, and he had seen many weirdoes, especially around the Time Square area. One would think that in the heart of this section of the city, loaded with sightseers, businessmen, and pedestrians of all types that the possibility of something strange would happen. With the diverse numbers of ethnicity, this was expected but what happened during this shiny bright day was one for the books.

'Alfo', as his friends at the Taxi Company had called him, came from a family riddled with drugs and mayhem. Fatherless for most of his life 'Alfo' pulled himself out of the gutter and worked odd jobs until he was old enough to get a driver's license. He had heard about the taxi-driver opening from one of the buddies at the corner market. He applied and got the drivers position. About a year after he started with the cab company, they filed for chapter thirteen. The company was saved temporarily by a firm out of California. The company cut back a lot of help and re-arranged new routes to enable the taxi firm to stay in business.

Alphonso did well with the new Management Company, until he was laid off. The owners of the cab company were forced to sell or go completely out of business. The new owners re-hired him with the promise of more hours and a chance of a percentage if he could increase business. 'Alfo' was thrilled about the program because since the new company had taken over, business had sharply increased. It was easy for him to make an extra hundred a month.

'Alfo' liked his job because he made good money and he was able to meet different types of people. He had overheard the conversation between Brad and the person that hired him to wait in front of Baetacom. After the drop off of the other guy, a couple of blocks from The Walton Hotel, he earned a great tip for rushing Brad back to the original pick up spot and the return trip to the hotel. As Alphonso was looking into his rear view mirror, he noticed his fare writing some sort of report, probably from his last meeting. Upon Brad's instructions, he stopped his taxi right in front of The Walton. His passenger got out of the cab. Alphonso noticed quickly that his passenger had left his briefcase in the back seat.

As he kept his eye on his rider he yelled after him: "Hey mister you for"--, Brad had disappeared! He uttered to himself "What the! He was right here--, well I'll be damned, he was right here!"

Alphonso looked at his right hand and realized that he was still holding his passenger's briefcase. "Well I'll be damned!" His only thought was to get the case back to the owner. The only place that he could think of was the hotel. Double-parked, he ran into the lobby and left the briefcase with the registration desk. "Some guy named Brad left this case in my cab and I'm sure dat he be headed here. He looked like he was in a big ass hurry. I can't find him, so here." He left the briefcase.

The clerk said, "Thank you we do have a Brad Warner. I'll be sure he gets this." The clerk took the briefcase.

Sweat was pouring down my face. It was so quiet that the only sound came from a highly pitched faint buzz that came from my brain. Darkness prevailed. There was no movement except from the strangely hazy glow from the distant red neon. It was getting smaller. It was diminishing in size! Was it vanishing, or was it simply moving away deeper and deeper into the darkest depth of the musty alley. I walked towards it again. Curious fear was gripping my heart as it beat with an irregular rhythm. No longer could I distinguish the lettering of the source of light. It now appeared as a dime sized smudge of ruby red. Curiously, its fluorescence saturated my mind to focus primarily on this crimson dot. The point of light increased in intensity in an unusual way. Its luminescence became a red sparkle once, then a muted glow, only to repeat this intensive dance. Repeatedly, this occurred, as I became came closer to the source.

Within ten feet now I had the urge to flee, but the need to have an answer offset the cold shivers that started at the neck down to the middle of my back. Cautious steps and quickened, uneven heart beat brought me a little closer. Each time the red glow intensified the reflection from its glare shone edges of a strange shape. The closer I got to it the shape came truer to form. Was it the mouth of the 'Cheshire' cat? Was something smiling at me? Closer now the edges of a mouth's sickening smile glinted back. Each time the glow grew in brightness that familiar sick, wanting to help, smile burned an image into my mind.

36

The red glow was the result of a deeply inhaled cigarette.
The familiar smile was created by the Bellman, Jules!
This still did not explain the dark.
This still did not explain the quiet.

Awakened in the room, I could see the flashing red light on the telephone. It reminded me of a terrible nightmare. I had a bad headache. I fell back asleep.

I was awakened again by a mad pounding at the door. Struggling to get out of bed, I called out. "Who is it, who's there?"

"It's me, open the door!"

"Who is it?" I asked.

"It's Willhelm. I need to talk to you!"

"Let me get something on, one minute." I muttered.

"Open up Brad!" He retorted. "Now!"

I worked my way to the door, at the same time threw on a robe. "Yes, Mister Rhorem." I knew I was in trouble. "I looked this over and kept what I needed!" He threw the briefcase onto the bed, as I grabbed a cold bottle of water from the cooler. "You stood me up!" He angered.

"Well I sort of blacked out." I rolled the cold bottle to my forehead.

"What the hell happened to your head?" Rhorem bellowed. "Look, you were trained never to be late and if you were, to call! You stood me up!"

"As I have tried to tell you, I had a problem. Getting out of the cab"—

He interrupted, as he turned his back to reach for water. "What are you talking about?"

"When I got out of the cab things went, well they all went dark and"--

Interrupting, he turned back. "Let's get back on track. Now you've saved time getting the contract signed, but I'm still mad about you missing our appointment. I do not want to have to replace you, but remember, we sell time management here. Understand?"

"But last night"—

He kept on. "Yes, well uh, you will need to make an appointment with the son of the owner. What's his name?"

I answered "Jeff, Jeff Foster."

"Yes, Jeff." He paused. "Set up a meeting and sell him on our program. He sounds like the type that would spoil the milk, if you know what I mean." His eyebrows furrowed. "I have to have everyone on the same page with this. When you sell one of these, you have to sell the whole company. It's sort of an insurance policy."

"Ok." I replied.

He continued as if he were testing my work. "Now when you are done with that I want you to work on that printing company. What was that firm's name?"

"Quick Print, they have twelve great locations with good volume but they need our help." I answered as if by rote.

"Yes Quick Print, a perfect candidate." He said this as if he were twisting a mustache. He went on. "Now get this job finished with Baetacom so you can start on the next. He started toward the door. "Now I don't mind a few drinks but let's not over do it!" He slammed the door quickly and left.

With a deep breath, I said to myself "What an asshole. I know for sure that his picture was in the dictionary under the asshole section."

He didn't even listen to my problem. It was as if he knew the answers to every question he had asked. The Old Man would be a tough one to live with. Thank God, that experience didn't fall into my lap.

I was glad I took the time to look into Quick Print, and more than glad I was able to get the rest of those papers signed. It might have been my ass right there and then.

I still cannot believe that last night was my imagination. A throbbing head told the story. Many questions remained un-answered. I was leery of leaving the hotel. I must admit I was afraid of another event. What was Jules doing there? This thing twisted my head and I couldn't put things together. I didn't have time to dwell on it right now. An appointment had to be made. A shower and a cold beer would help.

"Baetacom, may we help you?" Judy answers her telephone.

"Hi."

"Is this Brad?"

"What would you do if it wasn't?" I asked. "Do you normally know who is calling before you confirm?" I said in a joking way.

"I do when you have caller I.D., how are you?" She replied.

"Oh yes I forgot about that. I'm better now when I'm talking to you."

"What's the matter, didn't your meeting go well?" She sounded concerned.

"It's kind of a long story. The problem is I didn't make it. I would like to talk to you about it at, let's say, at dinner?" I awaited a response.

"Hey, you are a lot sharper than you look, just kidding." She laughed. "You didn't make it? Why, what was the matter?"

"Let me cover that at dinner. It's rather complicated, what do you think about trying that Italian restaurant next to your office? I can meet you there at 7:30. What do you think?" I was feeling very comfortable with her.

"Oh you mean Rodolphos, all these years, I've never tried that place, sounds good. In fact, I'm looking forward to it."

"Is that because you can't stop thinking about me?" I was testing the water.

"If you really want to know I"—

Interrupting, I didn't want a bad answer to spoil things. "I know what you were about to say. That sounds great. I am also anxious to see you." I cleared my throat. "I am very happy that you have accepted." I paused. "Remember when you asked me to talk to your brother?"

"Yes I do." She said.

"Do you think I could set up an appointment with him? Do I do that through you?" I asked.

"Yes you can but I'll have to confirm it. He is out of town however; he is supposed to call in today. When would you like to see him?"

"Do you think tomorrow would work for him?"

"You'll know when I see you tonight." She was very nice.

"Thank you, you are being very nice to me. I like talking to you. "I'll see you tonight." I prepared to hang up.

"Brad?"

"Yes?" I asked.

"Thank you for calling me." The receiver went click.

Wow- wow--- Wow! This made me forget what had happened the night before or was it the day before, whatever; I was in a great mood now. I could hardly wait for this evening.

I spent the rest of the day going over what I was to say to Jeff however my mind was thinking about Judy.

The telephone rang at 4: PM; it was Frank. "Hey buddy, you ok?"

"Frank, I have wanted to get hold of you!" I asked anxiously. "How am I supposed to keep in contact with you if I don't have your number?"

"Now take it easy Brad, I'm on the go but I have a beeper number to give you." He said apologetically. "What's the matter, I tried to call you yesterday I wanted to know how your meeting with The Old Man went. Did anything happen?"

"Yeah, a lot of shit happened. I blacked out or something. I banged my head, and I missed the meeting!"

"For Christ's sake, how could you let that happen? I mean, were you late or something?" He sounded upset.

"Frank, I had to go back for the briefcase. As far as being late, it was only a matter of minutes. Things went to hell after I got out of the cab. I don't know if I was hallucinating or if someone is playing a trick on me. I'll tell you Frank, I was in fear of my life!" I was agitated.

"Take it easy now Brad." He took a breath. "I told you before that if you were late, things would happen. That is not why I called. I called to tell you our investigation has, I have to say, 'stalled'. Any information that you may have, I'll need to know about it. That is why I'll give you the beeper number; it is going to be available to you day or night. I need to know everything that happens.

"What about this blackout that I experienced!" I yelled.

"I'll look into that." He was not convincing. "I gotta' run just make sure you report to me." He hung up.

Now what the hell was that? Frank sounded as though he was being preached to by Old Man Rhorem. I certainly did not

41

need two bosses. It seemed like no one wanted to hear about the incident that happened to me. If there was any information that I could become privy to, I suppose that I have to share it with Frank. From the way it looked, Frank was the only contact that was able to bring to light the nightmares to which I have been exposed. That is, if they were nightmares.

A sudden thought came to me so I decided to call the beeper number Frank had given me.

He called back within fifteen minutes. "This is Frank, Brad."

"Say, Frank, I think that the cab company, the bellman had set up for me, may be connected somehow. Could you find out how?" I was eager.

"Yeah, I already know that answer." He then questioned. "Why?"

"I was wondering why things happen when I get out of a cab. For example the last time I climbed out of one, things went to, well like I've been trying to say, dark." I went on. "It happened before just as"—

He jumped in. "The cab company that you are speaking about is Heritage Cab Company. The Rhortec firm took them over just before they went bankrupt."

I was surprised. "You mean that Rhorem owns the taxis too?"

"Oh yes." He sounded proud. "I sold that one, so I know about it." He told me to hold as he took another call on an incoming ring that was on call waiting. "Yeah, so yeah, he owns some other stuff too." He paused. "I didn't know you wanted to know about it, I guess I could have told you."

"Frank, if you need me to give you more information it would be helpful to know the score." I was wondering what else Frank had neglected to tell me. "What else should you tell me Frank, what other companies has he gotten, and"—

Interrupting he spoke quickly. "I'll go over that with you when I see you it's just that right now, I have to take this call. I'll be in touch." He hung up.

I stared at the telephone in my hand. "I'm getting tired of people hanging up on me." I said to myself, as I set the telephone on the base. I didn't think that I was getting the whole story.

During the second shower today, thoughts of a captivating conversation and dinner with the most interesting woman I knew will soon happen. Feeling a little nervous, I was careful not to make a mistake shaving. I wanted to look my best. Wearing the best slacks and shirt with a navy blazer, I found myself in the lobby awaiting a cab.

As I was catching the update news on the bar television from the hallway, I noticed Jules talking with someone that looked familiar. It was a bit of a distance from where I was standing. I couldn't make out the identity of the animated person to whom Jules was talking. Walking a little closer to them, the person that was pointing his finger at Jules face was Frank. Now why would Frank be here? Something smelled fishy about this whole thing. The taxi arrived. I had to think of this later.

"The Rodolpho restaurant please." The cab driver was the same guy from yesterday "Say do you remember me?" I asked.

Alphonso turned and instantly remembered and snapped his fingers. "Hey Brad! you gots' your briefcase?" He smiled.

"Yes, thank you. Do you remember what happened that day?" I scooted close to the front seat.

"Yes, brother, I dropped you off at that hotel." He pointed at The Walton as he drove away." You got out and you—you were gone." He gestured with palms up and apart. "Man, you vanished."

"You mean that I got out and you didn't see where I went?" I queried.

"Yeah, I guess you could say that. Where did you go anyhow brother?" He looked me up and down. "Hey man, you forgot your briefcase. I looked around and damned if I can find you. Like, you disappeared." He shook his head as if he was lost.

I shifted in the back seat and scooted closer. "Tell me what happened next."

"You don't remember?" he frowned.

"I wanted to get your story about things, that's all." Please go on.

"Well, after I found your briefcase, and I didn't look in it, honest; I figered that that thing was sposed to go wich you to the hotel. I takes it in there an' I givs it to the desk guy. Oh, I remembered your name from that other guy you was with. I kind of overheard you both talkin'." He was speaking with large honest eyes.

"I want to thank you for delivering it, and I would like to give you this." I handed him a twenty.

"Well thank you Mister Brad, I always tells myself that it pays to be honest." He smiled as he looked at himself in the rear view mirror adjusting his cap and showing posing teeth.

We arrived at Rodolphos. The cabby said that this ride was on the house.
We sat together at the rear of the restaurant; seeing her made everything okay. The restaurant was very 'Old Italian', with murals of Venice and Naples. I ordered a bottle of wine. She was very warm to me, as she expressed concern about the scratched bump on my head. I told her about what had happened after leaving her office. She was particularly concerned about the black out. Judy made me promise to talk to a doctor about it.

We finished dishes of the best manicotti and spinach ravioli that either of us had ever tasted. Sipping a wonderful Italian red wine, she looked at me with those beautiful eyes. "Brad thank you for a terrific dinner. It was excellent. Oh, by the way, I set up that appointment with Jeff for you. He was not thrilled about meeting you. He said that you should bring the contract with you so he could tear it up. – I'm sorry to have to tell you that."

My mind was on other things. "Let me talk to him, I'll do my best to show the benefits of the program."

She placed her hand towards me. "I was wondering, well, I was wondering if things do not go well with him, does that mean that you will stop seeing me?"

I immediately got the feeling of her closeness. "Judy, I haven't felt this way about someone in a long time." I took her hand. "I know this is sudden but I would like to see a lot more of you. I think there is some magic starting up here, no matter what happens with Jeff." I smiled as I looked into her eyes.

"I'll bet that you are just that magician too." She pulled me over to her and gave me an unexpected kiss on the lips.

We each enjoyed an after-dinner drink; she then drove us to her apartment. I was in heaven. The evening passed in bliss. She was warm, tender and loving.

She slipped on her robe. "Now before you go, I want you to call our family doctor. I am sure he can get you in." She handed me the telephone number. "You can call from here in the morning." Judy smiled.

The doctor was able to see me as a favor to Judy. I felt a little jealous until she mentioned his age of seventy.

I was introduced to Jeff that morning at the office. "Thank you for seeing me." He ignored my outstretched hand.
He turned to glance out the window. "Brad right?" I nodded. "Look Brad, I am afraid that my father made a mistake signing the contract with your company.

As you know, I have a vested interested in Baetacom. In fact, the reigns of this company will, in a few years, be turned over to me." I took some time to present the program to him but he continued. "I am going to cancel this contract. I just do not see how we could afford you."

I attempted to be firm. "Jeff, your company can't afford to not have this program. With every company that we have signed on, our management team has increased the profit structure."

He thought a second. "Get me a list of all the firms you have helped. I want to check them out. Obviously this contract has been signed without checking you guys out."

"I will have to get that list from the office." I was wishing that I had that report. Perhaps a copy of all of Rhortec's accounts would answer some of the nagging questions that were bothering me. "I'll check back with you, let's say, in a couple of days ok?"

He looked straight at me. "I don't give it much hope."

Walking past Judy's desk, I assured her of my loyalty, and told her that I would call her after the doctor's appointment. I gave her a little kiss on the neck.

From the hotel room, the call was made to Willhelm Rhorem to discuss the meeting with Jeff. "Hello, Will."

"Well what did you find out?" He spat out gruffly.

"It did not go well at all." I swallowed.

"Explain!"

"I talked to him about the whole program, bringing out every conceivable benefit to his firm but he wanted out of the contract. Finally, he agreed to look at a list of the businesses that you have worked with in the past. He required that you also furnish him with contact names. He wants to check with those firms personally."

He sounded mad. "He required?" I could hear the Old Man's fist slam onto the desk. "Nobody requires from me! Besides that, I don't give out lists! All information of the clients that we have done business with is strictly confidential. I thought you could handle this Brad." He huffed.

I thought about this comment. "How about listing a few of the clients? Maybe that would get him to go along. Some current ones would be good. Like for example, Heritage Cab."

"How the hell did you know about that?" He steamed.
I didn't want to tell him about Frank. "From, uh, the cab driver, I think." What was he trying to hide?

He was aggravated as he spelled out the words. We-Don't-Give-Out-That- Information, Brad!" He was breathing heavily now. "I know that you found that we took over The Walton Hotel. Now how do you figure this information would help? Smarten-up boy!"

Maybe I just got a little smarter. The Old Man did have something to hide and I'm right in the middle of it. I threw it back at him. "What do you want me to do now?"

He sounded resolved. "It seems that you have done all you can. I'll take care of it from here. Just sit tight until I find out what to do with you."

At least he didn't fire me. I'm not sure that was a blessing. I was getting sick of being reamed. I had to think. Things were getting rather thick. I decided to grab a drink at the bar downstairs.

On the way down, the elevator stopped at the sixth floor. My mind was so confused with the Rhorem ire that I mistakenly got out. At that time, the decision was made to take the stairs to clear my head. It was only six floors down. It would help to cool off. A loud familiar voice was coming from room 620. It was hard not to eavesdrop. I did an about turn and pretended to tie my shoelaces as I listened.

"He is not responding to it I tell you!" One voice said.

"Something has worked; he's blacked out a couple of times. That has every indication that it is working." The other one spoke as if he had a slight German accent.

"I don't think it took!" The familiar voice said. "What will happen if Willhelm orders you to?" Instantly I was all ears!

"We have to try to over-ride his programming to start again. He is very reluctant; there must be a natural block to the synapse. Don't you worry; I have done this many times in the lab. Just leave things to me Frank."

I was almost to the point of crashing the door to find out if they were talking about me, when I heard a rustling of the doorknob. Quickly trying the adjoining room handle, I discovered that the door was open. Dashing into the room and by leaving the door ajar, I was able to see into the hallway. If the other person was Frank, I didn't see him. Unfortunately, he had turned towards the elevator away from my position. Waiting for a few minutes, I had hoped that I could catch a glimpse of the other person in the room. He had evidently remained in the room. I tried to listen through the adjoining room door but there was silence.

Looking around the room, I noticed the key from the last person that occupied this suite. They must have checked out leaving their key on the dresser. I stuck that key into my pocket.

Something was definitely fishy. If what those guys were talking about what I thought they were, I needed more answers. Just the mere fact that they were talking about blackouts made me feel that I was being played for a fool. That is if I was the subject of their conversation, this may be the case. I hope not.

Out of the mood for a drink, I checked the hallway then went back to my room.

Judy called the next morning. I was very happy to hear her voice. Before I could tell her about what I had heard from room 620, She reminded me of the doctor's appointment. She also mentioned that a call came in from Rhortec's main office.

A luncheon appointment was made with Jeff for this afternoon. I was surprised that Willhelm Rhorem did not tell me about it. When I asked the details of the appointment, she told me that she didn't listen in on her brother's conversation. She laughed and said "At least not this time."

I told her that I missed her and she said the same. It made me feel good. We laughed. She had another call but before she took it, she made me promise to call after the doctor appointment.

One mile from Baetacom's office was located Doctor Carlisle's office. It was a mid –floor suite in a large brownstone building that looked as though it had been newly re-modeled. The top floor housed a working lab and office space. I was impressed by the warm atmosphere and kind receptionist.

"Thank you for seeing me in such short notice Doctor Carlisle." I shook his hand as he returned a very firm grip. He didn't look at all like a seventy- year old. "I'm Brad Watson? Judy Foster"—
He interrupted. "I know, I know." He waved a flat hand. "I've known Judy and the whole Foster family for, well before Judy and Jeff were born. She has told me about you and she said to take very good care of you." A big smile stretched from ear to ear as he guided me into one of his examination rooms.

"Now, Judy has told me about some blackouts you have been experiencing. Can you tell me more about what is happening?" He took out a legal pad and clipboard. "Please don't leave anything out."

I continued to explain the circumstances since arriving in New York. I spoke of the first time the blackouts had started and the second time after leaving the cab.

After the explanation, he arched his eyebrows from the clipboard "How much do you drink, son?"

For some reason, I trusted this doctor because I answered honestly. "To be truthful sir, the first incident was the day after I had been drinking more than I should have. The second time, however, no alcohol was involved. In the past, I have had hangovers but never have I been through this type of thing."

He was making notes. "Now you know as well as I do that excess alcohol will cloud your judgment and possibly cause hallucinations. I feel, however, that in this case there is something else going on." He set his clipboard down. "I want to get some vitals from you, and then I want to run a series of x-rays to get a better idea of things. What do you say?"

"That's fine," I said.

After taking blood pressure measurements and pulse, He asked. "Have you ever had an MRI?"

"I have heard of them but had never had one." I answered.

The doctor pointed his pencil at me. "I would like to do a CAT scan to see if we can get a good picture of what is going on. We can then see what other tests are needed." He turned his back to glance out the window, and then faced me. "If we don't find an answer then we can go further. The reason why I had asked you about an MRI is that we could compare an earlier scan with a current one.

"No I've never had one." I was intrigued. "What is a CAT scan?"

"It is computer axial tomography, or simply put, cross sectional images that are generated by computer from a series of x-ray scans of the particular area of the body."

I thought to my-self, ok? I didn't know what type of question to ask, except for one. "Can you do that here?"

"Yes, we can." He gestured towards the upper floor. "The best part is that I can get you out of here in under an hour. That is, if this is the only test that is needed." He was very assuring. "Now don't worry Brad, I'll get to the bottom of this, or Judy will have my head.' Again, that same broad smile appeared.

An hour and a half went by as I waited in a room. Doctor Carlisle entered. Brad could come in here please?" he motioned towards a white lighted wall that held an ex-ray. "Have you ever been shot with a pellet gun?"

"I was startled. "No, never, why?"

"There is something that is lodged by the area of the brain that controls the ophthalmic nerve. It is the size of two grains of rice." Pointing with his pencil, he showed the area. "I was thinking that you may have been shot with a pellet gun since the shape is this elongated form, just a moment." He opened a drawer and took out a strong magnifying glass. Examining the object a little closer, he took in a breath of air. "Wait a minute Brad, this is curious, and this is not a pellet.

This looks like some sort of, a uh, well it looks like some sort of computer chip!"

"A what?" I was stunned. Where the hell did that come from? I grabbed the magnifier and stared at this—THING. "I don't know how that got in there!"

"It's not very deep. I think that I can get that out with a small slit here." He indicated the simple procedure with a pointer. "All you'll have is a small bandage there." He pointed.

"Hell yes! Take that thing out!" That thing doesn't belong there, that I know, and it could be the answer to my recent headaches. "Can you do this now?"

"Yes I want to. I'll also send it in to be analyzed. Someone has installed this chip for some reason. I have an idea this is the answer to all your problems."

"There is no proof right now but it could also have something to do with the company I work for. Things have developed to make me wonder." So help me, I'll find out."

In ten minutes, Doctor Carlisle had completed the task with little or no pain. The clear pellet definitely looked man made with some sort of micro wiring connected to the smallest junction box or something. It needed further study to determine what it was.

One thing was for sure; I was pissed! Whoever did this thing to me was going to pay. I simply had to resolve this and the place to start was the hotel. I couldn't remember how or when it could have happened. The only thing that I could think of was if I had been slipped a drug and then taken advantage of.

The doctor and I had agreed not to tell Judy the whole story until results of the chip came back from the lab.

"Hi sweetie, I missed you. Thank you for getting the appointment to see Doctor Carlisle. He helped me with most of what happened."

Loving the way she answered the telephone, she asked. "What were the reasons for your blackouts?"

I carefully picked my words. "The 'Doc' is running some tests. After he ran a CAT scan, he may have found the reason for the problem. He is a good doctor; I can see that he is a worthy professional. He knows his stuff."

She sounded relieved. "That sounds great Brad. When can I see you?"

"That's one reason why I called, Judy, Could you meet me at Luigi's bar on the corner where the Walton Hotel is? I'll send for a cab to pick you up, let's say, at five?"

She quickly answered. "Absolutely yes!"

"Say, have you heard how the meeting with Jeff went." I asked.

"Not sure, he hasn't come back yet." She sounded concerned. "It must have been a good lunch, because he usually gets back to the office right away." She thought first then said. "Maybe he was talked into the program and took a little extra time with his appointment."

I was curious. "Do you know who he had the meeting with?"

"Actually, all I know is that a limousine picked him up in front of the office right on the minute they were supposed to meet. I was impressed. Your company knows how to run the red carpet don't they?"

"Yeah" If she knew what I was thinking she probably wouldn't have said that. "They do know how to pull out all the stops. The office has the resources that are not available to us lowly sales people." I said sarcastically, and then laughed. "Did you see who the limo driver was?"

"Yes, he said his name was Jules." She re-called "he seemed like the real smiles- type if you know what I mean."

Somehow, I knew the answer to my last question. "Yes I know that type."

"See you there then?"

"Of course." She answered.

"I have something I owe you any way."

She sounded exited. "What is it Brad?"

"A giant hug and kiss." Flowers with that would do well, I thought.

"Brad, I didn't think you were so romantic." She was toying with me and it was getting me exited

"Stop, you're getting me hot!"

Her telephone rang. "I'll do more than that Bradley. Gotta' go." She hung up.

Taking the stairway, I was able to get into my room undetected, but not before I stopped by room 622. There was a maid's cart in the hallway but I was still able to test the key card that I had picked up earlier. It didn't work. They must have changed the code on the lock when the last person checked out. They usually do for security reasons. That's ok, I had another plan in mind but it had to be done before the room was rented again.

It was getting to the time to meet with Judy, so I quickly freshened up and ran down the stairway, out the door and around the corner to Luigi's Bar.

"Hi honey." I was catching my breath as I spoke. "Sorry about being a little late." We kissed and hugged as if we hadn't seen each other in a year.

"Hey, that's alright, I was a little tardy due to heavy traffic. Things turned out in time anyway."

She stood back and took a good look. "Everything alright?"

"Yes I am much better being here with you." I pulled her towards me again.

She noticed the new bandage. "What is that new thing there?" She pointed to the bandage. "Did my doctor do that to you, or did you bump your head once more?"

"Yeah, that's just part of the test, I guess." Avoiding explanation for now was best.

"Oh, ok, I almost forgot to tell you Brad, my brother didn't show up yet. That must have been quite a lunch appointment."

Mulling this over I asked, "That's strange, isn't it?"

"Yes, like I mentioned to you before, he is always back in the office after lunch, unless he is out of town."

This was worrisome. The way things were developing, I certainly did not want anything to happen to Jeff. I dismissed these thoughts. I realized I was thinking the worst. "I hope things went well, just let me know when you hear from him."

"Oh, I'm sure he'll be in tomorrow." The waitress came over and brought our drinks.

Changing the subject, I asked. "Judy, what would you think if we were able to get another room at the hotel?" I took a sip. "It seems that the walls have eyes and ears, especially since I found out that Rhortec owns The Walton Hotel.

Something else has come up. Inadvertently I had overheard a couple of guys talking on the sixth floor. It seemed that the conversation was about the operations of the company that I work for. This has put some doubt about my future with Rhortec, so naturally, I would like to know a little more of the inner-workings."

"What would you like me to do?" She sounded intrigued.

"They know me well there, so I thought that you could rent a room for me today. The room that I want you to request is number 622. That room adjoins the room where I heard those plans." I was hatching this scenario as I spoke.

This cloak and dagger action had her interest. "Now how do I get them to give me that particular room?"

I thought about this. "Now if you tell them that room 622 has a special meaning for you, you could say that you are meeting someone there because of a memorable time you had in that room with him a while back."

She looked into my eyes and took my hand and we kissed. "You are really something you know?"

"You're not so bad yourself." She said. We kissed again. I left her there with the agreement to meet after she registered the room. I was anxious to see her and I could tell that she felt the same.

I was hooked. As she threw me on the bed, I knew that that had never happened to me before. We made mad passionate love. We had to remind each other not to make excess noise to avoid the neighbors in room 620 from hearing us.

Judy and I had gotten up at 4:00 AM. We were starving, so we grabbed breakfast at a place around the corner from the hotel. Due to the recent happenings that had surfaced, we did not want to be seen together in the restaurant at The Walton

She promised to call to give any news of her brother. Our relationship was growing better than I would ever have expected. Each time we met, it seemed that we were meant for each other. I had to admit to myself; I was falling in love.

Working the way back to my room, I was successful in not being seen. I noticed there was no message on the telephone as I tried to get a couple hours of sleep. This was impossible; my mind was working overtime thinking of all the things that were happening and all of the un-answered questions.

I had been tossing and turning until the telephone rang. It was Judy. "Brad, Jeff is gone!" She sounded desperate.

"I was afraid this was going to happen." I decided to tell her the whole story or as much as I knew so far. After she heard what I had to say, I continued. "Let me do some investigating and I'll get right back to you."

She said. I'm going to call in a temp to take care of these telephones, then I will call you back; you can tell me where to meet you.

"Please give me some time so that I can find an answer first." I pleaded.

"Brad, this is my brother." She added in a firm tone. "I won't take 'no' for an answer."

I knew not to try to talk her out of it. "Alright, Judy, when all that happens, call me at 622 at noon, ok? We can meet there and

54

no one will know. I'll use that extra key to let myself in and I'll wait for your call."

After splashing cold water on my face, the telephone rang again. I answered. "Yes, honey"—

A man's voice spoke. "Yes, honey? Brad my boy, what have you been up to?"

It was Frank! What rushed through my mind next was not to blow my cool. Somehow, Frank was involved in this whole thing and I didn't want to show my hand. In this way, I hoped to learn more. "Sorry Frank, I thought you were someone else."

"Hey, where have you been, oh I get it, you got lucky, right?" He laughed. "I've knocked on your door several times but no response."

I ignored his question. "What did you need Frank?' Taking a deep breath, I asked, "Did you get that list I asked for?"

"Uh, no, that information has been hard to get. I'll need a little more time." I could hear him stammer. Have you heard any more about Rhortec?"

"Not yet Frank, but I'll keep my eyes open and let you know anything I hear." I thought, two could play that game. "How about you Frank, any news?" I paused. "Where are you staying Frank?"

"Well, I know for sure, The Old Man does own the Heritage Cab Company"—

I interrupted. "That's old information Frank. Where did you say you were staying?" I was trying to pin him down.

"Uh, yeah, around the area, I'm trying to stay incognito, if you know what I mean." I could feel him squirming and realized straight answers were going to be rare from Frank. "Anyway Brad, please call with anything new, okay?"

Trying to sound up beat, I asked one more question. "Frank, why did you make the decision to leave Rhortec? I know you explained things briefly but if you could go a little more in detail I'd"—

"I'll tell you all that later but my beeper just went off."

"I didn't hear anything." I stated.

"Oh yeah, I have the damn thing on vibrate. It's always going off when I don't want it to. Hey, I gotta make this call; I'll keep in touch." He hung up.

I thought to myself; this guy is quick on his feet. I would like to catch him red handed. All of a sudden, I had a great idea.

55

I rushed down the back stairway and made it into room 622. As quietly as I could I dialed Frank's pager number, then hung up. I then rushed over to the inner door with an ear against it. When a beeper tone went off, I smiled and snapped my fingers quietly. I now knew that everything Frank had told me was a lie; and he was using me for information. For what reason, I didn't know. There was something that they were hiding and Frank and Rhortec were right in the middle of it.

The front door opened and there stood Judy. She looked worried. She explained that her brother Jeff had not shown up yet. Her father had not heard from him either.

I reached over to give her a kiss to try to console her. "Judy, we may be getting closer to an answer to this thing and I feel that Jeff's disappearance is connected to it."

I told her how I found out that Frank was in the next room and that he was trying to get information about what I knew. I suggested to her that we contact her father to have him put a hold on moving forward on the Rhortec deal. We accomplished all this while one of us kept an ear to the door. I knew that somehow we would find some answers.

She ordered room service as I stayed out of sight during its delivery. We were attempting to make things appear as normal as possible. All the time we were fishing for conversation from next door.

I learned long ago, to eaves drop, you place the bottom of a drinking glass to your ear and the other end to the wall or door, a person could hear just about anyone talking in the next room.

The telephone rang in the other room. Judy gestured for me to listen. I could hear Frank's voice. "No, I know he doesn't know anything."- Pause- "I don't know." -Pause-. "Willhelm told me to take care of it. When are you coming here?" -Pause-. "Well I'm not sure, that Baetacom kid is probably wandering around in the city. You know how the imagination works." –Pause- "Just as long as there is enough time lapses so the deal will go through." –Pause-. "Yeah, I know." He laughed. -Pause-. "I'll see you soon; we have to discuss what we want to do with him yet."-Pause-. "Hurry." He hung up.

I felt as though we hit the jackpot. There were things we still needed to know. At least we knew that Jeff's disappearance was because of Rhortec's tactics.

The telephone rang again. We were so busy talking that we almost missed it. "Shhh!" I said, motioning with exaggerated arm movements for Judy to pick up the drinking glass. "Listen." I whispered.

"Hello Mister Rhorem." Frank answered. –Pause-. "I'll take care of it." -Pause-. "But"— Pause-. "He called to cancel?" – Pause-. "I don't know where he is sir." -Pause-. "Yes sir, I will." - Pause-. "Jules sir." -Pause-. "Hello—hello.

Shit! We heard a slamming of the telephone and more cussing.

At least, I wasn't the only person that the Old Man commanded. It made me feel good that Frank was getting the treatment. "Sounds like Frank just got reamed." I said to Judy.

She asked. "What did he mean by saying Jules *"I believe that he was the limo driver that picked up Jeff at the office?"*

"I'm pretty sure that"—

Judy put her finger to her lips, and then pointed to the glass. "Wait."

We could hear Frank's voice again. "I want you to find him. The deal is going sour." -Pause-. "That is an order from Rhorem! – Pause-. This is not good you idiot! -Pause- "Don't fuck this up too!" The telephone slammed.

I looked at Judy. "Honey, I feel that I got you into all this and it's time to fix it." She could tell that I was getting mad. "Here is what I think we should do, I am going to run and get a cab and try to follow Jules. I need to find your brother and I need to find him fast. We can learn a lot about this whole thing by discovering where Jules will go." I placed both hands on each side of her face. "What I want you to do is to wait here and listen through this wall. We can find out even more from the person that comes to visit. I have got to go now because I don't want to miss Jules's exit from the hotel."

I got up and gave her a kiss. "I want you to be careful but most of all quiet. We do not want them to discover that we are listening from this room.

"Ok." She said, nervously.

"Get on the phone and have a cab meet me in front; ask for Alphonso and make sure you use my name. Also, put a pillow over the telephone. That way you can hear it but if I try to call and it will draw less attention if it rings." I pointed by jabbing my finger towards the next room.

"Ok" She frowned. "Be careful, please."

"I'll be back as soon as I can, you have the cell number. I love you." I told her this as I left the room. The hallway was clear as I rushed to the stairwell. My thoughts of her were quickly dashed as the urgency of what I was about to do filled my mind.

I jumped into Alphonso's taxi. He greeted me warmly. "Hi Mister Brad, where to?"

"Alfo, do you know the Bellman named Jules? He works at The Walton."

He looked at me in the mirror. "Sure do boss, why do you axe?"

"He is going to come out that door." I indicated the heavy glass doors at the hotel. "I would like you to follow him, sort of on the QT." I held up a fifty- dollar bill and he took it with a smile.

"You the man! I'll pull around the corner sos' he can't see me first." I had the feeling that he had been dreaming about this moment. No one had ever asked him to do that. Come to think of it, I have never asked a cab driver to do it. "Just like in the flicks," he said.

We both saw him at the same time. He was driving a black limousine that came up from the basement garage. "That's him, Alfo, go to work but don't let him see you.

He looked back in the mirror and winked. "Don't you worry with this heavy traffic and my drivin', he won't have a chance."

Jules started out going towards the Baetacom office. He then took a right and went two blocks. We followed with a car between us as he slowed. He looked as though he was looking to the left and then right as if he was watching a tennis match. He stopped a few times; double- parked and got out to search some narrow alleys. We stayed well enough back so that we would not be noticed as he continued the search.

He drove past some large buildings on the next block then stopped and parked. Stepping out of the limo, we could see him run towards a newspaper stand. With a handshake that seemed to

59

take an hour, his head was nodding while he asked some questions. The newspaper guy was pointing to what appeared to be the next block. With all the people that were blocking the sidewalk, it was hard to tell where the guy was pointing.

Jules did a U-turn that any sprint car driver would be proud of, especially in that big limousine. I looked at Alphonso and we knew that if we followed in that fashion, we would be seen. We were close to a corner so my driver had decided to go around the block. This was probably a good move. Who could lose a giant limo in one block?

Unfortunately, we did. By the time we were able to get around the block, that big monster was gone. Alphonso pulled into a cabby stop and pounded the steering wheel. "Shit, man he gone." He looked dejected. His first chance at a car chase and he blew it. To make it worse the car chase was a very slow one.

"Just stay where you are, you look down the street and I'll look up. He'll show. He couldn't hide that thing that quick." I turned around to watch out the back window.

What a city! I was amazed at all the life, the noises, the smells, everything and all we had to do was to find a black limo that stood out like an inflatable balloon at a Macys's parade. We were parked in a cabby spot massed in a cluster of moving human flesh.

A squad car with blasting sirens and flashing lights rushed past us at two miles an hour. I would hate to be in trouble during a rush hour in this town. Time would definitely be your enemy. Soon there was another emergency vehicle, trying to make its way to the intersection that was so plugged up that I doubted if you could shove a dollar bill in a crack.

"This is really jammed up; does this always look this way during this time of day?" I asked.

"Nah, sometimes I seen it worse. There must be an accident up ahead. Man you kinda' gotta' go with the flow; you know what I'm sayin?" Alphonso said as he tapped his fingers on the steering wheel. It was as if he was playing the bongo drums.

"You know I started to think of where that limousine went. What if it's parked in an alley and we can't see it from here?" I asked.

"Yeah, you might have a point boss." He turned to me, stroking his chin.

"It looks as though we will be stuck here for a while, can you loan me your hat, I want to take a look around. I'll be right back. Ok? I don't want to be recognized."

Alphonso handed over his hat. "You can use it but I want it back, 'sides it don't go with your color." He burst out laughing.

I pulled the cap down tight to cover my eyebrows and started to search the alleys. I finally spotted it. The monstrous black beauty was trying to get out into the street. The tinted windows did not allow me to see inside, so I walked closer to the front of the car where Jules was screaming at someone in the street through a rolled down window.

I caught a glimpse of a figure slumped in the corner of the back seat. The person looked as though he had been beat up. From what I could see, it was Jeff and he was in trouble. I had to think fast so I walked to the open window while I looked at my feet. I didn't want to be noticed. As soon as I was within an arm length of the big car, I slammed Jules right in the face. My fist screamed in pain. I hadn't done that since I was in high school. I looked up and saw that Jules was out like a light. He didn't know what hit him; it felt good except for my hand.

I reached over the door and hit the door locks. Running around to the blind side of the alley, I jerked open the door and halfway carried Jeff to the cab. To others on the street, it looked like someone was helping a drunk to walk.

By the time that I was able to get Jeff into the cab, the traffic loosened up a bit. We were able to drive past the limousine. I must have hit him very hard because Jules was in the same position as when I left him.

I told Alphonso only enough information to keep him from wondering. The most important thing to him was that he got his hat back.

I took him by the shoulders. "Jeff, Jeff, it's me Brad, tell me what happened."

All I could get out of him was that he thought he was going blind. Jeff struggled to speak. "Everything was as if it was at night." I shuddered when I heard that. I knew what he was going through.

I reached for the cell. Judy answered on the first ring. "I have him and he has the same symptoms that I had." I said.

She sounded very relieved. "Thank God, is he okay?"

I explained. "He looks a little roughed up. I have him in the cab and it would be a good idea if we could get him in to see your doctor. See if you can call, I'll rush him over there. He might need to stay for a while. How are things there; has Frank had company yet?" I was firing questions at her.

"No not yet. It's been quiet. -- I'm worried about you Brad."

"Listen, I'm fine now. We got your brother. Let me take him to doctor Carlisle and then I'll meet you in the room." I said goodbye and flipped my cell phone closed and I gave Alphonso directions to the doctor's office.

I reached for the door amidst shooting pains in my right hand. I wasn't that mad about it, knowing Jules got what he deserved. Doctor Carlisle helped me with Jeff as we set him up in an examination room.

I had to get back to the hotel, so I excused myself but promised that I would return. With the doc's quick examination of the hand, he assured that it was not broken. It sure felt like it.

Judy had moved the hotel's easy chair close to the inner-door that linked room 620 to 622. When she saw me enter, her smile seemed to light up the whole room. I missed her. It felt that I had been gone much longer than the three hours it took to find her brother.

She reached up to pull me down so that I could listen to Frank answer a long awaited telephone call. Over hearing the one sided conversation; Frank sounded upset as he spoke loudly. "Why, that stupid son of a bitch! I told him not to screw this up! Somebody's fighting us on this and I'm going to find out, or it will be my ass!" –Pause-. "No not now! I've got to question this ass hole; then we'll meet up!" We heard the clang of the receiver hitting the base of the telephone. Moments later, Frank's door slammed shut.

"It seems that Frank has left the building and the shit has hit the fans." I joked.

She stood and looked at me. "I missed you." We kissed. "How's my brother?"

"I think he'll be fine but I would like to talk to him and the doctor. While we have this break, let's go see how he is doing." I rubbed my hand.

"What's wrong? What did you do now?" She indicated the right hand and swollen knuckles.

"I'll tell you about that on the way over." I babied my hand into the right front trouser pocket. "Judy, you call the doc to tell him we are coming. I'll work my way down to the street to flag a taxi. Meet me in front. Oh, stop by the front desk and extend the rent on this room for a few days." I squeezed her shoulder with my good hand. "I missed you a lot."

She turned to me and looked deep into my eyes. I could melt right there. "Did you mean what you said?"

My skin tingled. "You mean earlier?"

"Yes, earlier, when you said you loved me."

It felt as though cupid's arrow had struck. "Yes." I grabbed her with both arms as our lips explored each other's love. At that moment, my hand didn't hurt anymore. The warmth and tenderness of her body led us to the bed; with complete purpose we undressed each other. I wondered as I un-hooked her bra, how two people could be so gentle yet so determined to prepare for the feeling of each other's bodies. She continued to explore as her stroking hand led me to her moistness.

Two stairs at a time, we reached the front door of the Doctor's brownstone. He led us back to a room where a disheveled Jeff Foster was resting. His troubled deep-set eyes were surrounded by dark sockets. It looked as though he was unable to focus his sight. His strength was sapped and was not the man I had known at our first meeting.

Still very confused he was able to give a slight smile as his sister touched his forehead and then kissed his cheek.

"He is going to be fine but he needs some serious rest. Let's leave him quietly; I would like to talk to you now, out here." Doctor Carlisle ushered us to his office. "Brad, thank God you were able to get him here as quickly as you did.

He is suffering from acute anxiety and confusion. I will know better about his condition after he is able to rest, I'd say, twenty-four hours. I have given him a sedative to help with that. I considered hospitalization but I felt that it would not be in his interest to move him right now. Besides, this is very quiet here. I'll be able to watch him tonight." He placed his hand on his knee. "That's one advantage of living on sight." He smiled.

"Did he say anything about what had happened?" I asked.

The doctor pursed his lips. "No I'm afraid that he is not able to answer any questions at this time. I didn't want to push him. Now with all that said, I want to show you something that is very disturbing."

He asked us to follow him to his x-ray lab. "I removed this." He showed us a clear pellet. "It's the same type that we found in you. It also has the same micro metal ends that were on yours."

"Has the lab report come back on my pellet?" I asked.

64

"No, not yet." He walked over to take another look at my hand. "But I hope to hear from them soon. You'll need to put ice on that."

We were in contact with Judy's father to explain the current circumstances. He was not happy. He did get hold of Rhoetec's main office to cancel the project and spoke directly to Willhelm Rhorem. With our insistence, he did not mention particular reasons except that he had some doubts about the program. That gave us enough time to gather more evidence from our stand in room 622. We still had no concrete proof. Once we found out, we felt that we could go to the proper authorities.

Bill Foster wanted more information before he made a determination so we all agreed to proceed with caution.

I stepped back into the hotel lobby, if for no other reason than to make an appearance. It was as busy as ever. Jules was not in sight, so rather than stick around; I decided to check my messages in the room. There were no messages. Judy said that she would call after an office visit to make sure that the temporary worker was doing things properly.

We felt that any telephone calls should be made to the room on the sixth floor. We didn't know how deep this thing went or if I was being watched.

The other thing that we were worried about was if the telephone in my room was tapped. We were taking every available precaution, so every time when I left my room; I made sure that no one followed me.

I wasn't careful enough. I awoke face down on a hotel carpet and with the worst lump on the side of my jaw. It felt as though someone hit me with a club. Lying in the middle of my hotel room floor, I slowly opened my eyes. Bending down above me was the biggest ear to ear smile that could only belong to one man, Jules!

"You can hit with one hell of a punch, so, I wanted to return the favor."

"How did you know it was me?" I rubbed my jaw.

"Well after you sucker punched me, a passerby described you, besides you were the only guy that had an interest in the person I had in the back seat. I put two and two together; here I am." He did a quick vaudeville impersonation of the end of a tap dance.

I put both of my hands up. "Ok you've got me, now what?"

"I think that we are even in the jaw department but now you owe me a favor." He rubbed his jaw. "I probably would have done the same if I was in your place."

"I'm sorry but—"

"Look Brad, I had wanted an excuse to leave this company since this Frank dude started throwing orders at me. He has downgraded and harassed me to the point that I can't put up with it anymore. I can make more down the street than here. It's just that I don't like being fired.

Ever since this hotel was taken over, it's been hell to work here. I don't like what you did to me but it is worse what they did. I believe in payback. That's the reason you're on the floor. Boy, you can sure hit." He was wincing as he shook his head, stopped and smiled with a nod.

I stood up. "Can you tell me what is going on here?"

"Well I don't know a lot but if it will help to get this Frank, I will."

"What do you know about the takeover of the hotel?"

Jules walked over to the bathroom sink and picked up a small baggie of ice. "Here, it's more than you gave me." He handed over the ice. "This new company forced the owner of this hotel out by getting him to sign a contract. An efficiency expert took over the management and soon after, he fired many people. I was one of the ones that stayed.

Business wasn't too good before the takeover but with just a few employees, we couldn't handle the business we had. We lost even more clients and Mister Walton Junior had to claim bankruptcy. This new outfit took it over. Funny thing though, Mister Walton disagreed with some of the contract requirements and tried to get out of it.

I was listening intently. "What were these requirements?"

"It had to do with always being on time. I'll tell you, they had me working a very long schedule; in fact, I was working a twelve-hour a day shift until today. The thing is, they didn't pay for the hours that I worked. The main thing was, the new management was a stickler about being late for anything. Since they did all this, business has been swift. This is an aggressive company that you work for."

"Yeah, tell me about it. What happened to the old owner?"

"He left for a couple of days and no one knew where he was. When he came back, he looked very sick. It was as if he had a mental breakdown. He didn't get a chance to cancel, anyway, right after the new company took over, and he died."

"He died?" That floored me! Do you know any more about the company?"

"Yeah, they took over the cabs out here, but I don't know any more about it. Oh yeah, they also own the meat outfit that supplies us with product."

"When you picked up Jeff Foster at Baetacom, where did you take him?"

"I took him to meet someone at a restaurant. I was supposed to pick him up at a certain time but he didn't show. A day or so after that, Frank said to find him. I guess the guy disappeared. If I didn't find him it would be my job, so I asked around the neighborhood."

"Does Frank know that I was involved?"

"Hell no, when I told him that I lost Jeff, he fired me. I wouldn't tell him anything then. The way that guy looked, well let's say, I didn't want anything more to do with this outfit." He helped himself to a beer from the bar cooler. "Thanks for the beer."

I nodded. We talked for a while longer. He offered his help if I needed it, as long as he wouldn't have to come back to The Walton. He was starting his new job in two weeks at another hotel. He did give me his contact number.

It was time to get to room 622. I wanted to make sure that Judy's call wouldn't be missed. She left a message for a make believe lover's name but I knew it was for me.

"Hi honey, how is your brother?"

"He is doing better- still resting. The doctor says that he should be fine in a few days. I was worried about him. Should I come over now?"

"Can you bring something to eat? Aren't you hungry?"

"I'll bring some Chinese and for desert, me." She giggled.

"You better hurry, see you soon." I hung up and then called Bill Foster to clue him in on the information I learned from Jules. I wanted to make sure that he was on the watch and to be careful, especially after learning about Mister Walton's death.

He told me that he had a message from Willhelm inviting him to lunch; he was probably trying to save the deal.

I told him not to return his call. We needed time to find out more. He agreed. He thanked me for finding his son, and wanted to talk when this whole thing was over.

Things were quiet next door. I must have fallen asleep in the easy chair. The dream I was having was real because of the next thing that happened. I remembered those juicy lips against my nose. Judy's lips were warm and sensuous against my lips. Her warm tongue was probing into my mouth. Waking up, I found her smiling over me as I took a bite of a sautéed mushroom.

I awoke, moaning pleasurably. "I'd love to tell you what you just made me dream of."

"Let's see, you were dreaming about being on a beach in Hawaii."

"Exactly!" I mused. "Let's eat."

"Heard anything?" She unpacked the pea pod beef.

"Not yet, this looks great." We ate and listened."

We talked softly as I filled her in on the information that Jules had given me. We were more determined than ever to resolve the situation. We were also worried that if we were caught eavesdropping, someone could get hurt. If what we thought was true about Rhortec, they would do anything to achieve success. We both felt that we might have enough information to go to law enforcement. Hopefully, they would find enough evidence to convict through the Federal Trade Commission. On the other hand, I felt compelled to protect Judy and her family, after all if it wasn't for me this would never have happened. I also knew that if things hadn't occurred, I would not have met Judy.

We were in constant contact with Doctor Carlisle and Judy's father by using the cell phone in the back room. We didn't want any noise to carry over to the neighboring room. We, again, took turns at the pass door. Listening.

A telephone's ringing drifted through the adjoining door only to sound muted as it signaled our inner ears. We stood frozen and alert anticipating additional information that could help to complete the puzzle. We hoped that it would be the piece we were waiting for. Would it be fragmented so that no sense could be made of it? Our only choice was to listen carefully.

We heard Frank. "Ten minutes, fine, don't be late." He hung up with
a light click.

I didn't know how long he had been in that room. I did not hear a door open or close. I whispered to Judy that we had to be very quiet.

I said softly. "Hand me that glass so we will be ready. I think Frank is going to have company."

We waited until a short knock was heard. "Hello, Gustav, you made it on time.

"Of course, you know better than that." Gustav quipped. "I don't think it took. I know you have tried to override his de-programming to start over. He is very reluctant; there must be a natural block to the synapses you have created. It's either that, or you did not do your job correctly."

"You don't know what you are talking about Frank." He said with his light German accent. "Technically my field is systematic manipulation of social and psychological influence. In simple terms, I control the elements of the subjects' social and psychological environments to eradicate undesirable modes of behavior. I am then able to instill or re-install desirable ones. I'm quite good at my work." Gustav sounded quite sure of himself, gloating at his sick accomplishments.

"But it's not working I said. Something is wrong." Frank retaliated.

"De-programming is the answer. I have been able to meld this program with the subjects own brain waves. The subjects aggravated brain waves then trigger this response, in other words, if a person is upset the natural electrical system will bridge, closing the circuit that shuts down his or her present situation. Darkness takes over along with hallucination.

"What if—"

"Let me finish, we have found that when the part of the brain that senses light is not used, the transfer of this unused energy goes directly to the part of the mind that controls the reality in thinking. The patient then hallucinates. What makes this different then a blind person is the programming. It comes as a total surprise and the brain cannot handle its sudden immersion in darkness Blind people know the reason for their disability.

Frank spoke quickly. "What if the implant is moved or becomes disconnected?"

"That is not possible, but another thing can cause it to malfunction." He was quiet for a moment. "This process is found to be a bit extreme so a buffer is installed. Usually the effect is over in about twelve hours." There was a pause.

Frank tried to interrupt. "What if"—

"Let me think!" There was a pause. "Did you not tell me that this, uh, Brad had two events?"

"Yes at least two."

"Then it must be working. As the patient goes into this other state, the natural thought would be to assign blame. In the case of Willhelms experiments that blame is time. The fact that being late for something creates the punishment it causes a dream or hallucinations. With the unusual high attention to the importance of time the brain will trigger the event. At the training sessions, we brainwash those trainees into believing that those that are tardy will be punished. Time becomes the switch as the anxiety grows to the point to set things off. Now if the subject has insulated the nodes of the device that we implanted, it could have a short life. I am not convinced that this is possible.

70

We heard Frank speak. "How did you involve time with Jeff, your last subject?"

"I didn't. I didn't have to. We simply did not use buffers."
"Isn't that dangerous?"

"It is extremely dangerous. I would be interested in examining him. Is he"--

Judy dropped her glass. It shattered next to the door making a loud crash. The conversation stopped in the other room and I thought I could hear whispering. We looked at each other as if our hands were caught in a cookie jar. Then the conversation between Frank and Gustav started up again.

I looked at her with relief. Gustav continued "Do you think that I can see him?"

"He is missing at this time." I heard Frank say.

"I thought you had Jules locate him."

There was quiet; no sounds were coming from the room. It was as if they were listening.

Gustav started again. "Did you say that you had Jules located?"

"Just a minute Gustav, I have to go to the bathroom."

It raced through my mind that we were in trouble. "Judy, something is wrong! Get into the bedroom!" We shut the door and suddenly the inner door to our room crashed open! We could hear the wood frame splinter! Like a herd of elephants, feet were everywhere. There were three voices! Frank was ordering them to search the room as we huddled in the bedroom. Luckily, as our door was flung open those that were searching didn't look in the bedroom closet.

"Here is a broken glass. It must have fallen from this chair. Let's get out of here; I'll have someone get this door fixed." Frank was saying.

The sweat was running down my face. I told Judy to wait until they had cleared the room before leaving the cramped space. From the sound of that door being crushed, I knew that we had to be even more careful so as not to be seen.

"Let's be easy now. I think that they have left." We opened the closet door and prepared to vacate.

"I left my purse on the coffee table. Do you think they saw it?"

71

"If I know Frank, I'm sure they did but did they put two and two together?"

I checked the front door. "Let's go, its clear."

We stepped into the hallway right into the barrel of a gun held by Jules. "Got you again, huh Brad?" He smiled that sick smile.

"You are a fucking liar!" He slugged me in the stomach that completely doubled me up! I gasped for air. I couldn't call him a liar again; I couldn't speak. Judy had screamed out when Frank held her back. Managing to struggle free, I smashed the side of Jules face with a backhand! He dropped; the gun flew as he hit the carpet!

Judy continued to scream arousing a big guy just two doors down. He saw that we were being accosted. He then ran down the hallway to intercede. By this time, Gustav jumped back into his room leaving Frank to face us. Jules wasn't smiling anymore because of a size fifteen shoe pinning his face to the floor. I yelled to Judy to get to the stairway, then to get a cab. "Wait in front!" I yelled that I would catch up with her.

I still didn't know the big guy's name but I was grateful that he came along when he did. Frank knew that he was out-numbered. He ran down the hallway as he escaped towards the elevator. Jules broke loose and followed.

I thanked the 'moose' while on the run. I had to make sure my girlfriend was safe. We met out front with no sign of the two. We jumped into the cab then took off in a hurry to put some distance between them and us.

My neck was sore from checking to see if we were followed.

There it was, a black Cadillac limousine making a corner and catching up to us. The aggressive way it was traveling, I was sure that Jules was driving.

"That wiry, smiling son of a bitch, he's right behind us!" I yelled! "You've got to lose him!"

The driver threw daggers at me through his rear view mirror. "Hey mister, I ain't no race car driver. I don't do that! I ain't loosin' my license!" He pulled over and told us to get out.

We swung the cab door open on the busy sidewalk and ran into a bar full of people. Moments later Jules entered; his eyes were wild! It felt like a horrible nightmare at the sight of him!

Grabbing Judy's hand, I dragged her through swinging, wing like doors to the kitchen. The cooks and waitresses scattered with the commotion.

Finding our way out the back into an alley, I pulled Judy into the street where we were lucky enough to flag a taxi.

We were safe. No way could Jules follow now. I felt stupid the way I fell for his story about being fired from the hotel. It was just a scam to find out what I knew about the operation. It was the same type of fraud that Frank had pulled on me when I first met him after his disappearance.

I knew that Jules wouldn't take this lying down. His eyes made him look as if he was a wild animal going for the kill when he followed us into the bar. I was worried about Judy's family and about how much Jules knew about her brother.

I had misjudged Frank. He was definitely pulling the strings and obviously, well trained by Willhelm Rhorem.

The criminal activities that led us to this point had to be told to the police. Searching my pocket for the cell phone, I discovered that I must have left it in the room.

This day was a blur, and I needed a cell phone. "Driver do you have a cell phone?"

"Sorry buddy, the company won't let us have one. All I can do is call the shack."

I turned to Judy. "We have to get to a telephone right away!"

She squeezed my hand. "We are only two blocks away from Doctor Carlisle. Let's stop there. I gave the address to the driver."

"Driver, do you know where that is?"

"We're on the way but keep your shirt on, this traffic is murder."

What normally would take a few minutes, ended up feeling like it took an hour.

It was slow going but curiously, when we arrived, there were several of the clinic's employees on the stoop milling around. There was a fire engine truck with lights flaring and another blasting its siren just turning the corner.

"What the hell is going on?" I yelled, out the rolled down window.

Someone in the crowd yelled back. "Fire alarm, someone' pulled a fire alarm!"

We jumped out of the cab and ran to a fireman standing by. "What happened?"

"We get some of these once in a while. Some jerk pulled this one for fun. I'd like to catch the bastard." He motioned to the group. "All clear, you can all go back to work." He then said something over his radio's microphone while heading towards his truck.

We looked around for the doctor and Jeff but they weren't on the street.

"Is my brother upstairs with the doctor?" Judy asked Irene, the clinic's receptionist.

"Doctor Carlisle is up there, he is making a call trying to find you."

We had puzzled looks on our faces as we ran up the steps. We found the doctor in his office holding a paper towel to his forehead.

"What happened to you doctor? Where is my brother?"

"Thank goodness you're here." He hung up the telephone. "The fire alarm went off so we evacuated the building. Turns out, it was a false alarm. Anyway, I took your brother out the back way and we were met by some guy that pushed me down to the ground. He took your brother. Boy, I must have scraped my head." He looked at the paper towel he was holding. There was a small amount of blood. "I'm sorry Judy but that guy took me by surprise."

"Can you describe him?" I asked.

"Yes, he said he knew you, I think he said his name was Jules."

We eyeballed each other as I shook my head. "Did he say anything else?"

"He told me to give you a message. He said, if you talk to anyone about what you know. It could be hazardous to his health."

"That son of a bitch!" I was pissed! "Doctor, which way did they go?"

"I don't know, when he shoved me down, they took off before I could get my bearings."

"Are you sure you're okay?" He nodded as a way of telling me, he was.

I turned to Judy. "They probably made their way back to the hotel. Doctor, I need to tell you what we have learned about this pellet. This implant activates an unnatural neural activity in the brain and- " I continued to tell Doctor Carlisle everything we had learned. "You will have to promise me that you will not tell anyone about this until we find that Jeff is safe." I grasped Judy's hand firmly.

She was upset. "These men have crossed the line when they took my brother. Their ruthlessness has caused them to kidnap Jeff and we have to make sure that he is not harmed!" Judy started to sob as I held her tight.

"We better inform your dad about this but let's make sure that he does not go to the police."

Later that afternoon, we worked out a plan that would try to put an end to this nightmare. Bill Foster agreed that we should not alert the authorities, at least, not until we exhausted our effort. We all, however, concluded that we would not fail.

Judy started at the hotel, acting as a maid. She was able to find a uniform in an unlocked employee's closet but unfortunately did not locate a master key to the rooms. She acted as a trainee, working with a woman that didn't question her. A number of rooms were checked but the maid that she was working with was assigned to a small portion of the hotel. The hotel had over two hundred rooms so the work was slow.

Judy was able to get into the room she was renting and found the cell phone that fell behind the easy chair earlier that day. One of the office employees at Baetacom rented another room under his name. That room became our home base as we tried to find the whereabouts of Judy's brother.

Later that evening, I tried to get into my old room but found the door lock had been changed. With a little help from my right foot, the room door was forced open and I found that all my items had been taken out. Clothes, computer, briefcase and all, were gone. I carefully went back to our new room without being seen.

We had to keep a low profile if we were to succeed in our plan. I don't think we would be as lucky this time, if we were found out. We were fortunate to have found the back staircase. Without that, we would have been caught checking the rooms, or moving about the hotel.

Bill positioned himself across the street from the hotel, reporting to me any unusual movements. He was particularly interested in those that matched Jules's or Frank's description that I had given him.

Early that next morning, I managed to make it out of the hotel using the service entrance. Judy, her father and I met for breakfast around the corner. We sat in a back booth of a busy merchant's cafe to discuss the events of last night. I should say

76

that we discussed the non-events of the previous night. We discussed the fact that we should not try to become any more aggressive than we have been. Getting caught now, would be very bad. These guys were playing rough.

All we needed was a break so that we could bring Jeff home. We could then go to the police.

I took Bill's place outside the hotel and at the same time went to a local store to get a change of clothing and other essentials to freshen up.

The entire time during shopping, the view of the front door of the hotel was in sight. I watched the busy front entrance as many people left or entered those heavy glass doors.

At this time of the day the street was full. It was rush hour. Pedestrians were briskly making their way back and forth in front of me with horns blasting from vehicles that seemed to travel at the speed of a snail. A few people that tried to cross the street had a difficult time trying to pass their bodies between the cars. Some had to wait until cars moved one direction or another to make enough space so a person could move. This whole menagerie occurred while you could hear yelling, cussing and just plain rude behavior. New York, it's a great place to visit but who would want to live here, especially downtown.

I have never seen so many yellow painted taxicabs in one block as this one. They were double-parked, as masses of people took their turn trying to hire one. Short whistles penetrated the morning as arms flew up to try to get that cabby's attention. This was high anxiety at its finest.

Watching this unfold brought a question to mind. If Jules was the one that picked up Jeff at the doctor's office what was he driving. In my haste, I had forgotten to ask that question from the doctor.

I dialed his number. "Hello Irene, this is Brad, can you put me through to the doctor?"

"He is with someone right now but he is just finishing up. How is it going? Oh, he is at my desk now, I'll connect you."

"Hi, Doc, how are you feeling?"

"Fine, Brad, I just got a little shook up is all."

"No success yet. The reason for my call was that I forgot to ask you a question about that fellow that knocked you down."

"Yes, go ahead, Brad."

"Do you remember what type of vehicle this Jules was in?"
"Why, yes, it was a taxi cab." He cleared his throat. "Why?"
"Do you remember anything about the driver?" I asked.

"Well, things were kind of hectic at that time. About the only thing that I do remember was that the cab driver was wearing a unique type of cap."

"Bingo!" I took a deep breath. "Thanks doc, I'll call as soon as we find out any more."

Alphonso, it had to be Alphonso! My next step was to find him. I had a few questions that could lead to finding Jeff! Although Rhortec owned The Heritage Cab Company, I knew that Alphonso was not part of the cover up and deceit of Frank's group.

He was a hard one to miss. His hat stood out in a crowd. From the telephone request to his arrival in front of shop where I had purchased new Levis, Alphonso was always on time.

"Hey, Mister Brad, where we goin'?" He was as enthusiastic as ever.

Hello Rodolpho, can I talk to you for a minute?"
"Sure, Mister Brad, what's up?"
"Could you tell me what happened at Baetacom yesterday?"
"Sure why don't you get in. Here sit right here." He patted the front seat and I sat down. "I drove out to Baetacom Company to pick up a guy and I brought him back to The Walton. There was a little pushing match between some old guy and that dude you was with the other day. He told me to go the back way, you know, through the alleys. He said I should do that to avoid traffic. That guy that I picked up looked sick or tired but I didn't axe no questions."

I was confused. "You know who Jules is, don't you?"
"Sure, he's the bellman at the hotel."
"Was he the person that was with you?"
"No, not him, the guy was the one that was with you the first time when I picked you up from here. I can't remember his name." You could see him thinking.

"You mean Frank?" I questioned.
"Yeah, dats the one!"
That had me thinking. "And, you brought them back here?
"Yeah."
"Can you remember anything else?"

"Yeah, it looked like this Frank guy was forcing the other one to go with him. I don't axe no questions because that hotel gives me a lot of business."

"Yes, I understand that. Now I would like to ask you another question."

"Okay."

"Has Frank or Jules ever asked you to do anything, well, shady?"

"Mister Brad, I don't axe no questions. I like to make money and this hotel calls me a lot for rides. As far as doing something illegal, I learned a long time ago that that's a not a good way to go. There is one thing that you should know, anything that happens in this cab that is a little off; I don't want to know about 'em Just about everyone here in New York will do things a little shady.

That's the way of life here. You gotta learn to live with it and axe no questions.

I picked my words carefully. "Alfo, I'm not talking about the everyday type shady things. I'm talking about things that a more serious, like kidnapping."

"Holly shit man, I never been with that!"

"I know that you think you have not done that, but there is a small group of people that operate out of this hotel that have made you become part of their plan." I could see his nostrils flare but I kept explaining. "These guys, Frank and Jules, have kidnapped my girlfriend's brother and have drugged him so they can take over his company." I tried to put things in simple terms.

"Hey that really pisses me off, man." He was visibly upset. "Since I was a kid on the street, nobody got away with that shit!"

"I was hoping you would say that. We have a plan that would get these people back but I would need your help. All I ask is that you not tell anyone about this conversation. I am afraid that Jeff, my girlfriend's brother, will be harmed if they find out that we have talked. I need you Alfo, what do you say?"

"Will it take time away from my job?"

"All you have to do is let me know what you see and hear. Once we get Jeff in a safe place, we can tell the police about them. That's the best way to get them back for putting you, me and Jeff's family in the middle of this mess."

We said goodbye as he taught me his handshake.

Frank was a conniving bastard. His deception of telling Doctor Carlisle his name was Jules was an attempt to hide the fact that he was involved in the abduction of Jeff Foster. By this time I am sure, that Gustav has discovered that Jeff's implant pellets have been removed. This created another problem of where they would strike next. If they realized that Doctor Carlisle was involved or held the evidence of that chip's removal, he could be in danger. Another thought would be that they have carried this take-over of the company far enough and any more exposure would bring more attention to them.

If I knew Willhelm and his company, they were determined to follow through, as if they were a bulldog on a bone, never wanting to let loose.

The three of us agreed that Alphonso was a great asset to getting Jeff safely back home.

Judy had been able to check out twenty rooms. It was slow going but she continued to search rooms while pretending she was a cleaning maid.

Bill was between the hotel and his office doing his part and Doctor Carlisle had been alerted to watch for any unusual activities at his clinic.

I decided to take the next step. It had only been one day since Frank found that we knew of his plan. I had felt confident that they would not try something foolish as long as I stayed in the crowd so I went to lunch at the hotel. I was greeted warmly by the restaurant staff that I was sure had no idea of Frank's doings.

There was a surprised look on the face of Jules as we caught each other's glances. He was walking by the restaurant opening. He stopped immediately when he noticed my presence. This was the first time that I had seen him without that twisted smile. I pushed my way clear of the table and a half- eaten lunch; I walked over to him. I approached him with a stinging smile because I noticed his bruised and swollen face.

My smile turned to seriousness. "I want you to return my belongings that had been taken from my room and I want them now."

His smirk returned. "How do you know that I took them?"

We were head to head but my voice was determined. "Don't bullshit me, Jules you are in a bunch of trouble. I want my stuff and I want Jeff returned to us immediately. If you don't, I'll see to it that you will pay. Those bruises that I gave you will only be the beginning of your problems."

He guided me to a quiet corner. "I only took your things to put them in a safe place. I'll get them back to your room, but what is this about Jeff? I don't know what you are talking about."

"I told you not to bullshit me Jules. You're in this over your head."

"I only do what I'm told, Brad. I don't know what you are talking about w-"

I grabbed his arm. "You're lying!"

He pulled free, at the same time, checked to see if anyone was looking. "I don't know what you are talking about!"

"Frank has Jeff in a room somewhere in this hotel. He took him from a doctor's office and said that you did it. That is kidnapping!"

"I didn't do that!"

It sounded as if he was telling the truth. I put the pressure on. "He has implicated you in this thing, you fool. You lied to me once to get information, how do I know you are not doing it again? Hell, I think I'll call the cops on this. They will straighten things out."

He seemed worried about me calling the police. "Wait, now, what if I can help to find out where he is?"

"Things will go better for you, you low life shit! I'm still not sure of you."

"Let me prove it to you. You go back to your room and in about two hours, you'll find your belongings will be returned. I'll try to find out about Jeff too."

"No, no. I have a better idea. I'll go with you now, for my things. I'll give you two hours to find Jeff, ok? Meanwhile, I'll wait in my room. I have some calls to make."

"Yeah, that will work too. Just don't call any cops about this."

I accompanied Jules to a security closet off the main floor and retrieved my things, then headed to my room. On the way, I dropped off my things at the other room that the Baetacom employee had rented yesterday.

In my old room, I looked around to see if I could find anything; it looked clean. Just before I left, I took the telephone off the hook. Looking down the hallway, I managed to find my way to the back stairway then to our safe room without being seen. I didn't trust Jules for one minute, besides if he had information about Jeff; he could leave a message on my cell phone.

Calls were made to Judy and Bill to keep them up to date. I asked Bill to go to room number 1027 my old room on the tenth floor. I wanted him to monitor it and report any movement. I used the next thirty minutes to shower and freshen up. Shortly thereafter, the telephone rang.

Bill Foster sounded stressed. "Brad, it's me, two men just kicked in your room door!" I could hear the elevator's floor signal over his cell. "From your description, it looked as though Jules was holding a gun! I saw it all because I was hiding by the ice machine vending area with a good view of the hall. You were right not to trust Jules!"

"I'm glad I wasn't in there! How close are you to me?"

"Just down the hall, unlock the door so I can get in. I'm nervous about being here!" He sounded out of breath. "Call Judy; have her meet us, we need to re-group!" He was saying the same words that I was thinking. Moments later we were all together knowing that it was more important than ever to get Jeff to a safe place.

We had to make sure of Jules's intentions. By leaving the phone off the hook, we were able to fool them into believing that I was occupying the room.

They played their hand when they kicked the door in. We decided that, we could take no chances of being caught.

In the middle of our discussing our plan, we heard some wild activity happening outside on the street. Car tires were screeching and loud yelling preceded ear-splitting sirens. The sound immediately grabbed our attention as we rushed to look out the window, down to the street. There was a mass of people gathered around someone lying on the sidewalk. Aid cars and a fire engine were making their way to the sight.

From our view from the second floor window, it was hard to miss the pool of blood building around the head of the victim. A police officer was pushing the crowd back from the body so that the emergency folks could attend to the body. It didn't look good. As the mass of on-lookers stepped back, we got a better look at the person lying there. Judy gasped at the recognition of the man. It was Jules!

A small group was huddled together while one of them was pointing to a room far above us. We were in shock! Jules had plummeted out the window from the tenth floor! It may have been that he was pushed! Either way, Jules was dead!

If Jules was a victim of Gustav's mind-bending brain switch, then Jules's death may be difficult to prove a homicide. Even someone as cunning as Jules could fall prey to the hallucination it causes. I know; it happened to me. It was devastating. The helpless feeling that it created took away all reality and reason. The anxiety that Jules was feeling may have set off the pellet's microchip to exacerbate the event.

Somehow, I felt that Frank was involved. He was the only person that I could think that would be capable of doing that. Frank was continually upset with Jules's performance in handling things. Every time Jules did a job, he bungled it.

The only way to tell if there was a pellet installed is by performing an autopsy. The pellet was so small that detection was impossible unless the doctor that did the postmortem was alerted to the fact that it might be there. The only way to tell if the chip was in was with a CAT scan, something not done in a standard anatomization.

One thing that rushed through my thoughts was that I might have been responsible for causing the anxiety to manifest itself in Jules's mind. Knowing that Jules was a 'rat' still did not justify that I might have had something to do with his death.

"I can't believe it!" Judy cried in horror. "We have got to tell the police what we know!"

Bill held his daughter. "Yes, we will. I don't want my son to end up that way." He glanced out the window with a sorrowful look. "Brad, I think we have waited too long. We have enough information to get these guys, don't we?"

I paced the floor. "Yeah, we do have that, but what about the warning that Frank has given us?"

I turned to look at both of them. "If we only had Jeff, I would feel so much better about it. This is going to bring many police into the hotel and I am sure there will be a lot of questions. Let's go down, meet them, and tell them what we have found. Surely, they will start a search, especially with all the information we have."

The telephone rang breaking the silence as our reflexes made us jump from the shrill sound. I picked up the receiver and made an indication for Bill and Judy to keep still. I said nothing, waiting for a sound from the other end.

"Hello?" There was a pause "Is that you?" There was another pause and then click, a hang up. I shrugged at the other two.

The telephone rang again, this time I simply said, "Yes?'

"Hey, Brad, is that you?" It was Alphonso.

"Alfo, thank goodness that was you. I didn't want to answer the first time just in case it was--"

"Hey, that's ok. You told me to watch for Jeff, well I seen him!" A siren's blast drowned him out. "Man you won't believe what's going on out here. This dude just jumped out of the hotel and th—"

"I know, we saw it all from up here!" I interrupted. What's this about Jeff?"

"I seen him, man he was in one of the hotel's vans that shot out of the underground parking ramp. See, I was waiting out in the cab to see if anything was happenin' and this dude smacked the sidewalk. Right after that, I seen this van comin' out of the parkin' garage. I knew it was him, 'cause that Frank guy was with him. We can follow him if you hurry, but not to worry there is a lot of traffic, he ain't gettin' too far too fast." Alphonso said with animation.

"We will be right down!"

"Ok, but hurry, this one is on me!"

By the time we had gotten to the outside of the hotel, the police had the street cordoned off. We took the back stairway and were able to get by the police to the awaiting taxi. This path avoided the questioning from the ever-present cops that were telling everyone to stay put. They were not allowing anyone to leave or enter the hotel. Our quickness had made it possible to get by them.

"I seen him go this way, past the alley on the left." Alphonso pointed to a dark dirty alley, with its garbage bags and dumpsters strewn about.

There were people living in old cardboard, appliance boxes, halfway down the alley. We were all looking in different directions trying to spot the hotel van. Our cab driver knew some short cuts so he drove down one of these alleys to avoid the traffic that was continually building. "I think he went this way." He turned left across two lanes of heavy traffic that lead back to the Walton. Alphonso had taken a roundabout course that put us ahead of the cars we were following.

Just ahead, a white van turned right at the light. Its tires squealed as it made the sharp turn. "Don't worry, that's not it." Alphonso said. "There was no printing on the side of that one."

Driving was tough as we continued to change lanes, and weave ahead to make as much progress as we could. I don't think anyone would be able to drive if they didn't own a horn. They blasted constantly with short and long beeps that made our apprehension grow worse. If it hadn't been for Judy, I would question the wisdom that made me want to come to New York in the first place.

Coming out of a side street another white van sped carelessly ahead. Alphonso's driving was amazing, winding his way through the mass of traffic that surrounded us. As the van turned the corner, Bill and I read the words aloud and at the same time, "The Walton Hotel" was printed on the side of the vehicle. The excitement was building as Judy's grip on my hand reminded me of the injury sustained from a knuckle buster that Jules received.

The anticipation of finding Jeff erased any pain that her squeeze may have caused. We were getting close enough to the van that I was afraid that we might be seen. I wanted to see where the van was going so that we could get Jeff to safety, but we wanted to make sure that Jeff was in it. Judy and I scooted down to the floor so that Bill could identify the passenger as we passed the van.

"It's him!" Bill rang out!

"Alfo, pull over as if you are picking up a passenger, and then continue to follow him to find where they are going. Don't get caught!" I yelled!

Now that we were behind the van, we raised our heads and sat upright back into our seats. It was clear that we had not been discovered. Alphonso stayed back far enough to ensure that.

One half-hour later, several turns and some fast driving, the van rested its wheels against the curb in front of a small warehouse. A step van with the words "Meyer Meats" was pulling onto the street through roll-up doors. As soon as the cargo van had cleared the path, the Walton van left the curb and pulled in. We sunk down in our seats as our taxicab pulled over on the opposite side of the road. With the poor light of the warehouse, we tried to recognize the two men getting out of the sliding door.

"That's Jeff!" Judy said.

"Yeah, and that's that son of a bitch, Frank." I mumbled, under my breath.

"What now, boss?" Alphonso asked.

"Look, I have an idea but we have to do it fast! Drive your cab directly under the door before it closes. Keep the cab running but leave it in reverse. Bill; make sure you hold this back door open after I get out. I'll locate Jeff and get him into the seat. Judy, you get up in front so we have enough room. Climb over the seat to get there. If anything goes wrong, get the hell out of here! I'll find my way back."

It's too dangerous, Brad!" Judy loudly disagreed.

"Not if we do this fast! I'll jump in, right after I get Jeff in here. No arguments now! Let's go Alfo!"

Bill started to resist but I held up my hand. "I got you into this and I'm going to get us out. Let's go!" I gave Judy a quick kiss, helping her over the seat.

When we drove in, I found Jeff sitting quietly on a shipping crate.

Frank was talking with some guy in the corner. He looked up in surprise as I grabbed Jeff by the arm dragging him towards the cab.

Frank yelled at me. "You! What the hell! Stop him! Stop him!"

I pushed Jeff into the back seat as Bill pulled him to safety! I was half way in yelling to Alphonso to go! Tires were smoking as he spun his wheels in reverse! I was able to get in but the back door hooked the jamb of the warehouse door and tore it off with a deafening crash of glass and steel!

"Shit, man!" Alphonso winced!

"Don't worry about that now!" I ordered. "Just get out of here!"

He slammed it into low and squealed his tires with blue smoke, leaving black rubber streaks on the cement. We were half a block away when I caught sight of the white van in pursuit. "He's coming after us, we have to lose him! These guys play for keeps!"

Frank exploded out into the street with his van as the rear end swung sideways! His tires tried to grip the pavement but he over- corrected and his van swung the other way like the tail of a mean dog. He straightened it up; showing the front grill displaying what looked like razor sharp teeth!

You could hear the taxi's engine whine as Alphonso stepped on the accelerator in an effort to lose the van. Frank kept getting closer until he was just a few yards behind us. With an intersection on our right, Frank attempted to ram us from behind. He was close enough to hit us when Alphonso made a fast right turn skidding around the corner! Bill had to hang on to me so I wouldn't fall out. It was a frightening experience sitting next to that huge opening. All I could see was fast moving, hard pavement!

Although the open door was causing a gale like force of wind against my face, I could feel the sweat over my entire body!

It was a little too fast for Frank to respond because he spun out in an effort to follow us! We had gained some time and it was our chance to lose him. We took another turn before Frank had a chance to catch up to us.

We were sure it was only a matter of time before we were seen. Our only chance was to hide the cab somewhere. Alphonso found that place. He took another right turn and then another to put us in a position one block behind Frank. One more right turn and we were able to see what direction he was heading. He was driving away from us at a very fast pace. Soon we would not be able to see him.

It was time to go to the police. The nearest station was about twenty minutes away.

Judy kept asking Jeff how he was doing. It was as though he had been drugged. This was probably the case. I wouldn't put anything past them. He was slow in answering questions, but at least he was answering them. This alone, was a good sign.

"They drugged me for Christ's sake. They first had me on a table and did this operation and"—

"We know, son. Now you are safe, you're not with them anymore." Bill looked into his son's eyes. "Why did they do this to you?"

"This Frank guy was trying to make me to not protest that contract. I overheard that they would take over the company." He was coming out of his haze.

"We know that Jeff," I said.

"I was wrong about you Brad, but not your company."

"Believe me Jeff, if I would have known about what their plans were, I would never have worked for them. "From what I know about them, they have taken over many firms. We are going to put an end to that right now. Thanks to Alphonso's driving, we were able to get you in a safe place. They had threatened to kill you if we had not followed their instructions."

"This German doctor put something in my head, I think.

"Hey, what about my cab, brother? I'm in some kind-a shit, now!?"

89

"Don't worry about that, Alfo, I'll make sure your company knows what happened here." I didn't have the heart to tell him that Rhortec also owned his company.

"I hope they buy it Brad. I 'aint never had no accident.

Bill put his hand on the back of his shoulder. "When this thing is all over, I'll make sure you have a job with our company, with a raise, of course."

"Yeah, ok. We're almost there. One more block."

Out of the corner of my eye a white van shot out of a side street and struck the opposite side of our vehicle! It spun us around in the middle of the street! It was Frank! He must have seen the police officer that was close by because he sped off through the traffic. The officer ran over to us to see if anyone was hurt. At the same time, he was describing the white van and the direction of the escape over his hand held radio.

"Are you sure you are all right? You folks are lucky that he hit you at the rear of your vehicle and not dead on.

"Judy, are you alright?"

"Yeah, that was a surprise. That really shook me up. Jeff, are you ok?"

"That woke me up!"

"You people, get out of the cab right away and get back from the cab. I think I smell fuel!" The officer opened all doors and helped us out to stay clear of the taxi.

A tow truck was called to clear the mess from the street and the Heritage Cab Company was called. This got Alphonso off the hook about the damaged cab. The street cop gave his report detailing the fact that the taxi driver was not at fault; this made Alphonso happy. He needed a new cab anyway. The officer questioned us about the accident and description of the van that hit us.

The rest of that afternoon was spent at the police bureau as we reported all we knew of the crimes we had witnessed. Kidnapping and a possible homicide were at the top of the list for the detectives that took our story. Several hours later we were released. An all-out search was on for Frank. They promised to let us know when they had him in custody. I knew that I could breathe easier when that was accomplished.

Jeff was feeling good by the time we were released from questioning but we decided to have Doctor Carlisle look at him to make sure he was back to normal. On the ride over to the clinic, we had to make sure that we were not being followed. We had had enough surprises for one day. I couldn't help myself from looking behind us to be positive.

Doctor Carlisle had finally gotten the lab results of the two pellets that had been removed. They were identical computerized switches. Now we knew the reason for those switches. They were an astonishing new technology that activates one set of sensory information for another in the brain.

When the anxiety of the individual was at a higher than normal level, that switch would activate, causing the optic nerve to shut down. The main reason for the intense training of new-hires was to keep appointments on time.

The old man put fear in your mind if you missed or were late for them. The penalties for doing so were devastating. That fear created the anxiety that enabled the switch inside the pellet to flip causing the scenario that I experienced to happen.

This whole, time restraint thing was created to enable Rhortec to enforce contracts that would soon take over new companies. I would still be in the dark if we wouldn't have worked so hard to find the answers.

This plan was very ingenious, no doubt, created by Gustav, who, was later found to be Willhelm Rhorem's brother.

Just as we thought, the case was turned over to the Federal Trade Commission and they, with the help from our information, found the other companies that Rhorem had appropriated illegally. Thank God we were out of it and we were no longer in danger.

Frank was apprehended and tried for murder.

******

Jeff was my best man when Judy and I got married. We hired Alphonso to drive our limousine and Bill Foster brought me in

91

to put together a time management program for Baetacom. I made sure that that all things were completed in a timely manner; this, in turn, made our profits soar.

END

MoreBooks!
publishing

i **want** morebooks!

Buy your books fast and straightforward online - at one of world's fastest growing online book stores! Environmentally sound due to Print-on-Demand technologies.

Buy your books online at

www.get-morebooks.com

Kaufen Sie Ihre Bücher schnell und unkompliziert online – auf einer der am schnellsten wachsenden Buchhandelsplattformen weltweit! Dank Print-On-Demand umwelt- und ressourcenschonend produziert.

Bücher schneller online kaufen

www.morebooks.de

VDM Verlagsservicegesellschaft mbH
Heinrich-Böcking-Str. 6-8   Telefon: +49 681 3720 174   info@vdm-vsg.de
D - 66121 Saarbrücken   Telefax: +49 681 3720 1749   www.vdm-vsg.de

Zeitfracht Medien GmbH
Ferdinand-Jühlke-Straße 7
99095 Erfurt, Deutschland
produktsicherheit@kolibri360.de

Druck:
CPI Druckdienstleistungen GmbH
im Auftrag der
Zeitfracht Medien GmbH
Ein Unternehmen der Zeitfracht - Gruppe
Ferdinand-Jühlke-Str. 7
99095 Erfurt